The Pierced Hearts Duet

CHOOSING Us

Dedication

For anyone who needs to believe in love again.

Acknowledgments

There are so many people I would like to thank!!

HEATHER MOSS: Thank you for being my right-hand woman and always being there for me. Our friendship means everything to me. You knocked it out of the park with these covers, Yoda!! I am forever grateful for you.

BELLA MOSS: Thank you for inspiring little girl Bailey Button with your giggles and smile.

SILLA WEBB: As always, thank you for your speedy edits and always making the time for me.

ERIN NOELLE: I love you forever and ever.

WESTON BOUCHÉR: You were the perfect muse for Aiden. I couldn't have asked for a better model to work with.

DESI & STEVEN PERKINS: Thank you for inspiring the Beauty And The Beast Scene in the book.

Muffins:

Lily Garcia: Thank you for all the laughs and quick feedback you always provide and for keeping it honest with me. You're the best.

4

Emma Louise: Thank you for always proving quick feedback! You are a godsend. Anytime I ask you for

anything you always deliver and help out where and when you can. I appreciate you so much.

Jennifer Pon: You have been one of the best alphas I've had on this book. Thank you so much for your honesty and boo boos. You have helped bring Choosing Us to life.

Jessica Laws: As always, you're an angel. Thank you so much for the quick feedback and the suggestions you bring anytime I ask for them.

Leeann Van Rensburg: Thank you so much for always sharing anything and everything I post. The way you run my street team and help out is amazing to me. You are one of the best people that have come into my life.

Louisa Brandenburger: I love you so much. I am praying hard for you as well. Thank you for being here for me. I can't tell you how much I appreciate that and you.

Michelle Chambers: You are such an asset to my team, and I can't thank you enough for all that you do.

Nicole Erard: You were another alpha who helped bring Choosing Us to life as well. Thank you for everything that you do. I can't thank you enough.

Alphas & Betas:

Betty Lankovits: Thank you for all the teasers and laughs that you bring into my life. I can't thank you enough for it. You're an amazing soul. **Michelle Tan:** Welcome back, I missed you. **Tammy McGowan:** Thank you for coming through with the feedback and suggestions! I really appreciate it so much **Michele Henderson McMullen:** LOVE, LOVE, LOVE you!! **Carrie Waltenbaugh:** Anytime I send chapters you always jump on them so quickly. Thank you so much for that. **Mary Jo Toth:** The amount of boo boos you always find amazes me. Thank you for always being so wonderful and helpful. **Ella Gram:** You're the sweetest beta ever. Thank you for always giving me your honesty and your feels. **Tricia Bartley:** I always look forward to your emails because you always give back the best feedback, and it makes me laugh every time. **Kristi Lynn:** I missed you! Welcome back. **Patti Correa:** You're amazing! Thank you for everything! **Maria Naylet:** Thank you for always giving me your honesty! You're amazing, and I'm so lucky to have you on my team. **Deborah E Shipuleski:** Love you, babe. **Kaye Blanchard:** Thank you for everything! **KR Nadelson:** I missed you, welcome back. **Georgina Marie Kerslake:** As always I love you. Thank you for loving my babies the way you do. **Ashley Reynolds:** Thank you for all the feedback and suggestions. I can't tell you how much it helps me. **Chasidy Renee:** Thanks for it all! **Danielle Renee:** You're amazing!! **Marci Antoinette Gant:** I love you so much, and thank you for everything!! From my street team to reading for me. **Dee Renee Hudson:** You're the best, girl. I love you so much. Thank you for everything. **Misty Horn:** Thank you so much for helping me bring Aiden to life! **Nohely Clark:** Your feedback is always amazing!! Thank you for everything. **Ashley Singer-Falkner:** Thank you for all your quick feedback. You have helped me so much. **Mary Sittu-Kern:** You were so much help. Thank you! **Sanne Heremans:** I love you so much! Thank you for all the help! **Kris Carlile:** Your feedback was amazing! Thank you for being so honest! **Elena Reyes:** I love you.

M's Good Ol' Girls:

Jamie Guellar: Thank you for running my street team along with Leeann Van Rensburg, and always being there for me. Amanda Roden, Amy Coury, Ann B. Goubert, Ashley Sledge, Beverly Gordon, Chantel Curry, Christin Yates Herbert, Corie Olson, Darlene Pollard, Donna Fernandez, Jessica Laws, Keisha Craft, Leeann Van Rensberg, Lily Jameson, Marci Antoinette Gant, Melinda Parker, Michelle Chambers, Nicole Erard, Nysa Bookish, Ofa Reads, Paula Deboer, Rhonda Ziglar, Sarah Polglaze, Shawna Kolcznyski, Tara Horowitch, Terri Handschumacher, Tracey Wilson-Vuolo, Tiffanie Marks & Vanessa Reyes!!!

6

Words cannot express the gratitude I have for you!!! I wish I could personally hug and kiss you all. Thank you so much for pimping my books the way you do. I can't thank you enough for it. You ladies are amazing to me. I hope to meet each and every one of you!!

Bloggers:

Most of you have been with me since I started my writing career over five years ago. I can't thank you enough for always supporting me every way you can. I appreciate and love you so much. I couldn't do this without you. I love you.

My VIPS & Readers:

Thank you so much for loving my babies the way that you do. You guys bring so much happiness and love into my life, and I love you so much. I couldn't do this without you. You mean everything to me!

CONNECT WITH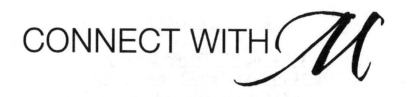

WEBSITE
FACEBOOK
INSTAGRAM
TWITTER
AMAZON PAGE
VIP READER GROUP
NEWSLETTER
EMAIL ADDRESS
YOUTUBE CHANNEL
SPOTIFY

MORE BOOKS BY M
All FREE WITH KINDLE UNLIMITED

EROTIC ROMANCE

VIP (The VIP Trilogy Book One)
THE MADAM (The VIP Trilogy Book Two)
MVP (The VIP Trilogy Book Three)
TEMPTING BAD (The VIP Spin-Off)
TWO SIDES GIANNA (Standalone)

CONTEMPORARY/NEW ADULT
THE GOOD OL' BOYS STANDALONE SERIES

COMPLICATE ME
FORBID ME
UNDO ME
CRAVE ME
EL DIABLO (THE DEVIL)
ROAD TO NOWHERE
ENDS HERE
EL SANTO
EL PECADOR
LOST BOY

NOVELLAS
KEEPING HER WET
KEEPING HER UNDER THE MISTLETOE

AIDEN

"I just don't know who you are anymore!" she screamed out with pure hatred dripping from her voice.

In her eyes.

In her fucking soul.

Her fists slammed into my chest with a hard thud, but I barely wavered. I'd take every blow, every yell, every single goddamn thing she delivered.

Her pain.

Her sadness.

Her desire to let go and just be.

It was all clear as day, glaring right at me.

The fear in my mind grew at a rapid speed, corrupting the only vacant spaces left of my being. The unease festering inside me was far greater than anything I'd ever known or felt.

It took over as I stepped toward her, instantly blocked by an imaginary wall she had built so high, it would simply crush her the moment I tried to knock it down.

Caving us both in.

"Get away from me! Just get away from me!"

She was slipping further away from the life we fought so hard for.

Everything we wanted.

Everything we needed.

Everything we prayed for time and time again was disappearing like a thief in the night.

Willingly taking the love of my life with it.

"Bailey … please … please don't say that. I'm begging you…" I extended my hand, but she immediately pulled away as if the words she spewed were in fact our reality.

Leaving me far behind.

I ran my hands through my disheveled hair, yearning to rip it out of my head. "Bailey, ple—"

"No! No! No! No!" she wholeheartedly repeated, placing her hands over her ears. Backing into the wall with nothing but her sobs and desperate pleas filling the small space between us.

Wrecking the fuck out of me.

"I don't want you anywhere near me! Go away! Just go away!"

I couldn't breathe.

I couldn't fucking breathe.

"Bailey, just calm down! Calm the fuck down and let me—"

"I don't want you near me! I don't need you! I want nothing from you but for you to leave me alone!"

"Bay, you know I can't do that," I strongly conveyed, trying to steady my tone. Compose myself, catch my bearings, knowing it would help bring her back to me in the end. "Beauty—"

"Stop calling me that! That's not my name!" She reached for the first thing in sight and chucked it at me. Her rage completely taking over.

I let the glass hit my shoulder, hoping it would help her find truth through the lies.

"I don't know you anymore! Why can't you understand that I don't want anything to do with you! Nothing!"

"Don't push me, Bay. You don't mean that. You don't fucking mean that. Please, baby … don't do this … don't fucking do this to us…" I pleaded with my hands steepled out in front me.

Praying.

Surrendering.

Relinquishing defeat.

My white flag was up. My goddamn flag was raised up high, flowing adamantly through the storm.

"Just stay away from me," she murmured so low, I could barely hear her. Narrowing her gorgeous eyes at me with an endless stream of questions splitting through her unsettled gaze. Making it difficult for her to focus solely on me.

On my voice.

On my presence.

Her.

Me.

Us.

"Aiden—"

"Please don't leave me, Beauty. Please…"

I took an agonizing step toward her. "I." Two more slow steps. "Love." Another two brought me inches away from her mouth. I resisted the desire to claim her lips like I'd done hundreds, thousands, millions of times before.

A lifetime of kisses.

I love you's.

You're mines.

Instead, my eyes stayed fixated on her face. My core seized tighter, my knees got weaker, my body ached, remembering the reassuring symmetry of her heart beating against mine.

"You, Bailey Ashlyn Pierce. My girl, my wife, my best friend, my whole fucking heart." Grabbing her face in between my hands, I yearned for her to feel me.

To see me.

To love me.

The man who would die for her.

It didn't take long for our bodies to close the emotional and physical distance between us. From her mind to her heart, to every goddamn bone in her body, I knew she felt it. There was no way in hell she couldn't sense the effect I always had on her.

The effect she'd always have on me.

"You're all the same. Don't you get it? You're one of them. You're just one of them to me, Aiden. That's all that's left. Don't you see?"

I gripped onto her face. "To Hell with that, Bay. I'm your one and only. I'm your home."

"There's no peace for me in that house."

"I know, you took it all with you."

Her body trembled, her strong, hardened composure weakened with each word that escaped from her mouth. "Why do you keep hurting me?"

I grimaced as if the wind had been knocked right out of me. "I would never hurt you. Never. I'm here, Bailey." My grip shifted toward the nook of her neck, tugging her toward me, bringing her heart against mine. "I'm right here."

She hadn't let me feel her warmth, her security, her heart in what felt like an eternity.

"*This* is where I belong. Where I've always been since we were seven-years-old. I'm a part of you. I need you to hear me screaming out for you. I still need you, Beauty. I'm lost without you." Pulling her hair away from her face to look deep into her eyes, I said the only thing that was true.

The only truth I ever knew.

"*I choose us*, Bailey Pierce. I will always choose us. No matter what. I. Choose. Us."

She consciously jerked back from the weight of my words.

My girl was at a loss, and I had nothing left to lose.

"It's you and me against the world, baby. It's always been you and me against the world. You know that, Bay. You do. Just come back to me … please. *I can't live, I can't breathe… I can't go on without you.*"

She didn't say a word, not one fucking word. She just stood there, looking at me. Searching for the man she once knew. Her resolve was slowly breaking, but I couldn't take it anymore.

I broke down. I bawled, pulling her back toward me, and to my surprise she let me.

"If I did anything right in my life, it was loving you. Do you understand me? You were the beginning of *everything* for me. You will forever be my always, Bay, I only need two things in this world. *You* and *us*. Just *you* and *us*, Bailey." I leaned forward, setting my forehead against hers, taking a deep breath, trying to gather my thoughts.

My emotions.

My fucking memories.

"I'm trying, Bay. I don't know what else I can do. Please don't give up on me. On us."

"Aiden … please."

I peered up at her as tears started spilling down the sides of her beautiful face, one right after the other. She didn't even try to hide them, she let her emotions flow freely. Wanting me to see the part inside of her she thought died long ago.

"Just take me back, baby. Please… God, just take me back to the night we first met," I faintly uttered near her ear, hanging on by a thread.

Hoping she realized the significance in what I just said.

As soon as her eyes filled with fresh tears, I wiped them all away. Not knowing where to go from here. She held my gaze until the sensations became too much for her. Lowering herself onto the edge of the bed as her chest heaved for her next breath.

In one swift movement, I fell to my knees in front of her and clung onto the back of her neck. There was no way in hell she could keep me away. Before she even realized what was happening, I was holding her delicate frame in my strong and steady arms. Kissing away the tears on her face as they fell to the floor between us. She stirred beneath my lips, her body shuddered under my touch.

Giving me hope, strength, the reassurance I needed to go on.

"Aiden, please…" Her mouth quivered. "Just let me go."

"I won't lose you," I breathed out against her lips. "I have seen you in so many different ways, and I have loved you in each one of them. For better or for worse, Bay … for better or for worse, I will love you."

She sucked in a breath, and our mouths parted in sync with one another.

"You're my answered prayer, Bailey. I will love you until I stop breathing, until the last seconds of my heart beating, because you are my beginning and my end."

"Aiden," she rasped an eerie tone, causing shivers to course down my spine as I knelt before her.

I ignored the looming essence that wrapped around my neck like a noose. Simply sucking the life out of me. Shutting my eyes, I softly kissed the corner of her mouth.

Recalling every memory.

Every sentiment she ever lured out of me.

Every instance I fought for what was mine.

15

CHOOSING US

What do you do when you meet your soulmate at seven-years-old?
You give…
You live…
And you love…
Until you hear the words, "I just don't love you anymore."

Putting an end to us.
To you.

To me.

For now and forever.

AIDEN
Then: Almost eight-years-old

"Baby," Momma whispered like it hurt her to speak.

I sat on the edge of her hospital bed and grabbed her hand, holding it as tight as I could. My warmth comforting her cold, clammy skin just like I knew it would. She loved when I did that, giving her a little squeeze so she'd know I was there. So she'd know she wasn't alone.

Momma didn't like being alone.

"I love you so much, Aiden. Do you have any idea how much Momma loves you?"

I smiled, laying my head on her tummy. Cuddling closer, listening to the soft thumps of her heartbeat. "I know, Momma. I know," I calmed her, knowing she loved hearing that too.

She looked so tired. She always looked so tired now. Spending more time sleeping than awake every day. Sometimes she had good days where she'd laugh and ask how my day was, but I couldn't remember the last time she was awake enough to say anything to me. Making me super sad and lonely.

I really missed those days and couldn't wait for them to come back again. To have my momma back like she used to be before she got sick. I hated seeing her sick, I hated it so much. Every night and sometimes during the day, when the sun was shining bright, I would pray to God to help her feel better, so I could have my momma back. Playing with me, talking to me, paying attention to me like she always had.

"Momma! Momma! Momma! You have to chase me!" I shouted, trying to get her to run after me faster.

"I am chasing you, Aiden! And as soon as I get you, you're done for, Little Man!"

I laughed, throwing my head back. Almost tripping over my own two feet.

"Gotcha!" She giggled, tackling me to the ground.

I threw my body around as soon as her fingers started tickling under my chin. I hated getting tickled there the most.

"Momma, stop!"

"Who's your favorite girl?"

"You, Momma, you!"

"Good, remember that when girls start coming around."

"I hate girls!"

She stopped tickling me, smiling and laughing. Finally letting me catch my breath.

"Well, baby, girls are going to love you, and I'm not ready for any of that. You can never leave me, okay? You stay Momma's Little Man for life, alright?"

I nodded, sitting up. "I won't leave you, ever. I swear with my whole heart. But you won't leave me either, right, Momma?"

"Mommas don't leave, Aiden. Mommas never leave," she replied, brushing the hair away from my eyes with a sad smile on her face.

"So then only dads leave?"

"Oh, Little Man ... dads aren't supposed to leave either."

"But you said my daddy left."

We never really talked about him. I never met him, she said he left before I was born.

The troubled look on her face made my chest hurt. It was one of the reasons we didn't talk about the man that much.

"I'm sorry, Momma, I don't want to make you sad." I gave her a hug, wanting to make her feel better. She always said my hugs were the best and the cure to anything in this world.

"I don't need a daddy, Momma. I have you. You're all I need, I promise."

"I'm sorry you don't have a daddy, Aiden. I never wanted you not to have a daddy. But don't you worry, Little Man, moms don't

leave. They never leave. I promise you, I'll be with you forever, Aiden. It's you and me against the world," she repeated for what felt like the hundredth time. *"Just me and you against the world, Little Man."*

The words played out in my head again and again, remembering the last happy memory I had of her before she got sick. I didn't mind taking care of her, though. It's what you did for the people you loved. You took care of them.

No matter what.

"Momma, when are you going to feel better, so we can play? Do you think you'll feel better next week? Joey, Felix, and Tyler's parents won't let them play with me anymore, cause you're never around to watch us. They won't even let me play with them at their houses where their parents can watch us. Something about me not thinking or acting like a seven-year-old boy should, cause I'm always taking care of myself. And you're making me grow up too fast." I rolled my eyes. "Whatever that means."

"Oh, Aiden…"

"It's okay, Momma." I shrugged. "I didn't want to tell you, but I'm really missing my friends. So do you think you might feel better by next week?"

"Oh, Aiden…" she repeated, looking up at the ceiling with tears in her eyes.

"Please don't cry. I don't like it when you cry."

It was what I hated the most about telling her what people were saying. My teachers at school were always asking me questions about my home life. All sorts of questions that had nothing to do with them. Most of the time I just lied to keep them from asking me again, but it never worked. Sometimes the principal would even call me into his office with the guidance counselor, and that always made me really nervous.

They said everyone was just looking out for me because they were concerned. I guess all eyes were on me since they found out I was walking to and from the bus stop by myself. The walk wasn't even that far, not as far as the small grocery store on Rubles Road.

Now that was a very long walk, and the lady behind the counter always had the saddest eyes when she saw me. Kind of like

Momma's right now. I didn't like it when anyone was sad, especially when I was the cause.

It was the worst feeling in the world.

Maybe I did grow up faster than the other kids in my class, but who wanted to be a little boy anyway?

Not me.

I was Momma's Little Man, and I took my job of being the man of the house very seriously. Besides, it wasn't that bad. I didn't have a bedtime, I ate when and what I wanted, and I didn't have to answer to anyone like my friends did with their moms and dads. Sure, sometimes it sucked having to take care of myself, but Momma needed me, and that was just the way things had to be.

But it was being alone that got to me the most, especially now that my friends were taken away from me too.

"Momma, it's not a big deal. I'm sorry I made it sound bigger than it was. I guess ... I just miss you, that's all. I don't like not having anyone to talk to or to play with. It's not fair I'm being pushed away for having to take care of us. Ya know?"

"I know, baby. You're such a good boy. You've always been my good boy. You know that too, right? Please, tell me you know that, Aiden."

I nodded, hating the sound of her voice when she was sad. "Of course, I know, Momma. I'm your Little Man. I'll always take care of you. So please don't cry anymore. You know how much I hate it."

"But, baby ... I'm sick—"

"That's why you're here at the hospital," I reminded, smiling big and wide for her. "To get better. The doctors and nurses are gonna make you all better, so you can be my momma again. As soon as you are out, we have to go to our favorite ice cream shop. Go for walks in the park, watch movies in your bed with the popcorn you love just like we used to. Do you remember, Momma? All the fun things we used to do before you got sick? I can't wait." I nodded, smiling even wider. "I've been praying really hard too. Really, really hard, just like you showed me."

As soon as I finished talking, she jerked back and shut her eyes. More tears fell down the sides of her face, only making the pain in my chest worse. I wanted that feeling to end, to finally be gone and never come back again.

I reached up and wiped away her tears, careful not to move any of the tubes coming out of her nose like the doctors said. Except she wouldn't stop crying. She'd never cried this much before, and my heart had never hurt this bad before. It wasn't easy seeing and feeling her this upset, unable to do anything for her. Unable to stop the pain that always took her away from me.

"Momma, don't cry. Please ... everything is going to be alright, you'll see. I promise. I'll protect you. I won't let anything happen to you. Your Little Man is here with you."

I spent day and night by her side these past few days, even though I wasn't allowed to sleep at the hospital. The nurses knew I had nowhere else to go, so they let me stay.

"Baby, more often than not when people get sick, it's because God has other plans for them."

"What kind of plans?"

"Plans you won't understand because you're just a little boy."

"I'm a Little Man, Momma. I'm your Little Man."

"I know, baby, I know." She slowly placed her arm around me, and I snuggled closer to her cold body. Her skin felt frozen like ice, not like the warm, soft heat I was used to every night.

With a huge, deep breath that I felt in my tummy, she added, "But even my Little Man won't understand this. Because, Aiden, I barely understand it, and I'm not seven-years-old."

"I'm almost eight," I reminded, smiling through the pain. "My birthday is coming up, and all I want is for you to get better. That's all I'm wishing for, Momma. Nothing else."

"Aiden ... I need you to listen to me. I need to have faith that you'll be okay without me. Because this is all I have left to give you, baby."

"Without you?" I frowned, looking up at her. "Where you going?"

"I'm going to Heaven, baby. And one day we'll be reunited. I promise, Aiden. I promise you'll see me again. I swear it."

My heart sank. Tears started forming in my eyes. "But I don't want you to go to Heaven. Stay with me, Momma. Just stay with me. I don't care if you're sick. I'll take care of you like always," I cried right along with her, unable to control the feelings I'd never felt before. My whole body hurt so bad.

"I love you so much, baby. Don't ever forget that. Not for one day."

Why did it feel like she was saying goodbye?

"Then I'll come with you to Heaven. If that's where you're going, then that's where I'm going too. We'll go to Heaven together."

"Baby, as much as I love you … you can't come with me."

"Why not? I wanna go to Heaven with you, Momma. Just take me with you … please…" I bawled, feeling like my heart was exploding in my body like the fireworks on the Fourth of July. Except this wasn't fun.

I couldn't control my tears, and I didn't want to. She had to understand I needed to go with her.

She couldn't leave me behind.

I'd be all by myself with no one to love me.

"I promise I'll take care of you in Heaven, Momma. I'll be your Little Man anywhere we go. As long as we stick together, everything will be fine. You and me against the world, remember?"

She caressed my cheek. "You can't come with me, baby."

I pulled away suddenly angry, snapping, "You can't leave me, Momma! That's not what mommas do! You said that at the park! You said mommas don't leave like dads do! That's what you said! Remember? That's what you told me!"

"Aiden, please calm down."

"No! You can't leave me! It's you and me against the world! That's what you've always said to me! Remember?! That's what you've always said!"

"I will never leave you," she choked out, coughing over and over again.

I threw my arms around her neck, holding onto her as tight as I could. Showing her, she wasn't leaving me. I wouldn't let her, she'd just have to take me with her.

Momma, you're all I have.

You're all I've ever had.

Her breathing came out in quick, short puffs, like she couldn't catch her breath. Whispering, "I will always…" she gasped for air. "Be here for you… Just because." She started coughing, gasping for more and more air. "You can't … see me, doesn't mean … I'm not here."

"It's not fair. It's not fair that this is happening," I rasped, fresh tears soaking her green hospital gown. Struggling for my next breath, I asked, "Who's going to tell you everything is going to be okay, Momma? Who's going to tell me? Who's going to cover my eyes during the scary parts of movies? Who's going to tell me they love me? I don't have a daddy! Or an aunt or a grandma! I don't have anyone but you! Who's going to help me back to sleep when I have a bad dream? Who's going to be there for me when I get home from school? Who, Momma, who if not you? Don't you see? Don't you get it? You're all I have! You're all I've ever had! There's no one else but you! So either you take me with you, or you stay with me! You stay with me, Momma, because that's what you said, that's what you promised! Mommas don't leave! You have to remember! Please, you have to stay with me!"

My body fell onto hers. Crying for what seemed like hours, just lying there. She tried everything to calm me down. Weakly humming "Smile", like she had since the day I was born.

Smile, though your heart is aching.

Nothing could make me smile, laugh, or be happy. I'd be nothing without her.

Nothing.

"Everything is going to be okay, baby." She rubbed my back, holding me close, as close as possible. "I love you more than anything in this world. I have loved you since before I even met you, my beautiful boy. With those bright blue eyes that have always been able to see inside my soul. What we share, the love, the bond, the connection between us … it can never be broken, Aiden. No matter where I am, no matter who you're with, we're together in here." She placed her hand over my fast-beating heart. "You'll find someone who will always be there for you."

"I will?"

"Yes, I swear it."

"How do you know?"

"Because, Aiden. I'll personally send her your way. I promise."

All I could do was nod because I couldn't find the words to tell her how much I loved her.

23

How much I needed her.

How sad and alone I would be without her.

What's going to happen to me?

It wasn't until she placed her hands on the sides of my face that it felt like I was dying too. "Listen to me, Aiden Hazel Pierce, because I will only be able to say this once. I need you to remember you can be anything you want to be. Do you hear me? You do not let what happens next in your life define who you are. Do you understand me? You make your own path, baby. Your own path and bright future that I know you're capable of. I need you to promise me you will do something amazing in this world. You will make something of yourself that will have me so damn proud of the man you've become. Because I'll be right here, baby." She nodded to my heart. "Watching, listening, cheering for you until the day we can be reunited again. I'll be waiting for you with open arms, my beautiful boy. Now prom—"

"Momma." I tried to pull my face away, but she held me as tight as she could.

"Promise. Me."

Even though I didn't want to, I nodded. My eyes dropping to the ground as I did.

"Let me hear you say the words."

"I promise."

"I need you to mean it, Aiden. Please, for me. Mean it for me."

"Okay." I looked up at her. "I'll do it for you, Momma. I promise, I'll do it for you."

She smiled through the tears, and before I knew what was happening, the machines around her started going off. "I. Love. You, babyyyy—"

Beep. Beep. Beep.

"Momma."

Beep. Beep. Beep.

"Momma!"

Beep. Beep. Beeeeeeeeeep.

I shouted, "Somebody help! Somebody please help her! Don't leave me, Momma! Please don't leave me!"

"Get him out of here!" one of the nurses ordered, rushing into the room.

"No!" Hands immediately touched me everywhere, carrying me out into the hallway. "Take me with you, Momma! Please just take me with you!" I screamed as loud as I could.

Fighting for her life.

But mostly…

Fighting for mine too.

AIDEN
Then: Almost eight-years-old

I'd been sitting in the office the nurse put me in forever ago.
Walking back and forth.
Wanting to see my mom.
I just wanted to see my mom.
Why was that so hard?
Why were they making this so hard for me?
Didn't they understand, I needed to be with her?
Everything would be alright if we were together. She needed me.
She needed her Little Man.
Didn't they know I was her Little Man?
"Where is my mom?!" I screamed toward the locked door. "I want to see my mom! You can't keep me in here! She needs me! My momma needs me! Open the door!" I slammed my fists against the hard wood with as much force as I could. "Just open the door and let me see her! Please! Just open the door!"

I couldn't hold back my feelings. I couldn't control the pain, the sadness I didn't understand that was taking over me.

It was hard to breathe, to see, to feel anything other than the mad feelings in my heart.

"I want my momma! I just want my momma! Please! Please! I'll be a good boy! I promise, I'll be a good boy, just let me see her!"

My fists pounded against the door harder and faster until it hurt so bad, I had to stop.

Until all I saw was Momma behind my tears.

Until all I wanted was to give up and wait for her to come find me.

I needed her to hold me in her arms and tell me everything was going to be okay. That everything was going to go back to the way it used to be before she got sick. Before she stopped playing with me, before *she* stopped taking care of *me...*

Before.

Before.

Before.

"Please," I begged, losing all the fight I had left. My feet slipping out from underneath me, bringing me down to the cold floor.

I was so tired.

"Dear, God. Heavenly Father. Please let my momma be okay. Please let me see her. Please don't take her away from me. She's all I have. She's all I've ever had. I can't lose her, please don't let me lose her. Please, God—"

When I heard the keys turning in the lock, I stood up quick. Thinking my prayers had been answered. Waiting to see my momma walk through that door.

With my heart pounding out of my chest, I greeted a woman I'd never met. Blurting, "You're not my mom."

She didn't look at me at first. Instead, she nodded to the nurse who pulled me in here, and then to the tall, scary man I didn't know, before finally looking me in the eyes.

The look on their faces made my belly ache and my muscles squeeze tight, but I still didn't let it get to me.

I had to stay strong for my momma.

The woman with kind eyes got down in front of me, putting herself at my eye level.

"Hi, Aiden. My name is Misty, and I work for CPS. Do you know what CPS is?"

I swallowed what felt like something mushy in my throat, slowly shaking my head no. Trying to breathe in through my nose and out through my mouth, like Momma showed me when I was scared.

"Well, I work with kids and their parents, Aiden. I make sure kids are safe, having a place to live and getting everything they need. Do you understand?"

I nodded because I couldn't get the words out.

"Can you tell me a little bit about what happened today?"

"I don't know." I shrugged. "Can you take me to see my mom? Please. I just want to see my mom."

For a second her eyes moved to the other people in the room before she said, "Aiden, I'm going to need you to come with us, okay?"

"Are you going to take me to her?"

"No, I'm not, but I will take you somewhere that has people who will take care of you."

I stepped back, getting away from her. "I don't want to go with you, I want my mom. You're not my mom. You can't take me anywhere."

They taught us stranger danger in school. I knew all about it.

"I know you want your mom, sweetie, but she's..." She stopped talking, taking a deep breath. "I'm so sorry, Aiden, but your mom is gon—"

"NO!" I instantly covered my ears and shut my eyes as tight as I could. "I can't hear you! I can't see you! I want my momma! I want my momma! Get away from me and go get my mom! I want my mom! I hate you! I'm not going anywhere with you! I want my mom now!"

Strong hands grabbed my wrists, yanking my hands away from my ears, and I lost it. Going after anything I could see in the office, I destroyed everything around me. I ran around the office, that I now saw was the hospital's playroom, my feet stomping everywhere I stepped.

Ripping pictures off the walls...

Throwing toys out of the buckets...

Shoving magazines off the tables...

Screaming, "You're not my mom! You're lying! She's not gone! She promised me she'd never leave! She promised me! Moms don't leave! Moms aren't supposed to leave!"

My eyes were blurry from my tears, and my body was filled with so much hate.

For them.

For her.

"I hate you! I hate you!" I yelled, repeating it over and over.

"Aiden, calm down!" Misty ordered from somewhere in the room.

"I want my mom!"

"I know, honey, but your acting out doesn't help with anything. Please calm down!"

"I'm not going with you! Not now! Not ever!"

Hands touched me again, carrying me up and holding me down onto someone's shoulder.

"Stop! Don't touch me! You can't touch me! I don't want to go with you! I want to see my mom!"

A huge sadness laid down on my heart.

I felt lost.

Like nothing or no one could help me find my way out.

I kicked.

I screamed.

I fought.

Trapped in the arms of a strange man I didn't know.

Being taken to a life I didn't want.

The man hurried out of the hospital with the nurse and Misty running beside him, and no one did anything. Like this was normal or just another day at the hospital where they took kids away from their moms daily.

He opened the door, throwing me into the back seat of a car that was parked out in front. My body rolled around on the seat as the door slammed closed behind me.

"Please! Don't take me!" I reached for the handle, yanking it as hard as I could, but it was locked. "I don't want to go! Please!"

I kicked at the door, the window, the backs of their seats, but nothing helped.

Nothing worked.

"Mom! Momma! Take me with you! Just take me with you! You promised! You promised me that you would never leave me! It was you and me against the world!"

It wasn't until the car started driving away from the hospital that I knew my life would never be the same again.

I had no one to take care of me.

To love me.

To make me feel like I was home.

My saddest days were still coming.

Because now...

I was really alone.

"Aiden—"

I turned my face toward the window and shut my eyes, ignoring Misty who was in the front seat with the mean man driving.

I hated him.

I hated her.

But mostly, I hated my mom.

It didn't feel like a long time had gone by, when I felt the car stop and the engine turn off. The last thing I remembered was kicking and screaming, then nothing. I must have fallen asleep, too tired to keep fighting. It didn't matter anyway. I left my heart, my tears, everything back at the hospital with my momma.

The car was quiet and dark, the moon and headlights were the only lights in the night as far as I could see.

What will happen to me now?

The door opened out of nowhere, making me jump, and the big man nodded for me to get out. "Come on, son, we're here," he said, reaching out his hand for me.

"Where am I?" I asked, only looking at the tan house with a gate around it. Pushing his hand away, I stepped out onto the grass by myself. "This isn't where I live."

Misty looked at the man the same way she did back at the hospital before getting down to my level.

"Aiden, since your mom is gone, I can't take you home. This is where you'll be temporarily, until I can find you a permanent placement."

"What about all my stuff? My clothes, my toys, my games! Momma's books, our pictures on the walls, my favorite pillow and blanket with Ninja Turtles on them... Momma bought them for me before she got sick! I want all my stuff! Please get my stuff. I promise I'll be good! I won't fight. I promise. I just want my stuff."

"I'm sorry, Aiden. I can't do that. We'll find you some clothes and toys here, alright?"

"No!" I stomped my foot and tightened my hands. "It's not the same! You can't do this to me! You can't take all my things away from me, like you took me away from my momma! I want my stuff, and I want it now!"

"Aiden," she whispered in a low voice, "I'll try to grab some of your things for you, but I can't make any promises, okay?"

"But I want to go with you! Take me with you! I want to see my house! You won't pick out the right things!"

"Yes, I will. Tell me three things you want the most?"

Was she lying?

Could I trust her?

Could I trust anyone?

"Only three?" I replied, surprised.

"I'll try to grab as much as I can, but give me three items so I can at least grab those things for you."

I bowed my head, giving up. She wasn't going to take me with her. She wasn't even listening to me.

Would my voice ever be heard again?

"I want the picture that's on my nightstand by my bed. It's a picture of me and Momma from when I was little," I told her, wiping a tear from my cheek. "She looks really happy. She was always really happy, Misty. Even after she got sick, she always tried to smile for me. Sometimes it looked like it hurt her, but she did it anyway. Do you think she is still in pain?" I asked the question I'd been holding in, remembering her cold skin on mine.

A feeling that would never leave me.

Misty grabbed my chin, making me look up at her with new tears in my eyes, as I sucked them back down.

"What else?"

"My Ninja Turtle blanket and pillow. I know that's two things, but can they count as one?"

"Yes, they can count as one." She nodded. "Now name one last thing."

"Momma's favorite book to read to me, *On the Night You Were Born.* She always read it to me at night time, to keep the monsters away." I looked into her eyes. "Who's going to keep them away now, Misty?"

She frowned as if she could feel what I was feeling, never taking her sad eyes from mine. "Your momma is in Heaven."

"But Heaven is so far away."

"I'll be here too."

"You will?"

"Yes, Aiden. I'm going to request to take over your case and be your caseworker from here on out. I have some pull with my supervisor, and I know I can make it happen."

"Does that mean you'll take care of me? I can stay with you?" I asked, needing someone to love me.

Her bottom lip moved fast and her eyes watered, shaking her head at me. "No. You can't stay with me, sweetie."

"But you just said—"

"I know, but you don't have to stay with me for me to take care of you. I'm going to place you in a good foster home, Aiden. I promise."

"But I don't want to go anywhere else. I want to go with you. I'll be a good boy, Misty. I promise. I'll be a Little Man for you, like I was for my momma. Just take me with you. Please, Misty, just take me with you," I begged for what felt like the millionth time that day.

"Aiden, I can't take you with me and do the work I do for other kids. But I do need you to be that Little Man like your momma taught you, okay? Can you do that for me? Can you do it for your momma in Heaven?"

I ripped my face out of her hand. "I hate her. I don't want to do anything for her."

"I know it feels that way now, but I promise it will get easier."

"When? When will it get easier, Misty? When you put me in a foster home I don't want to be in? When I become someone else's problem? And you forget all about me like Momma has. Is that when it will become easier? Because that doesn't sound easier to me, Misty. It sounds harder!"

"I know it does, but it will take time. I promi—"

"I don't believe you! You don't know me! You don't know anything about me! You're just trying to get me to do what you want! I'm not stupid!"

"Aiden, I know you're not stupid. I know you're scared—"

"I'm not scared. See ... you don't know anything. Let's just go. I'll follow you inside, so you can place me in a foster home where the monsters can find me."

"Aiden, that's not—"

32

"I don't want to talk to you anymore!" I went around her and started walking toward my *temporary placement* like she called it.

I didn't need her.

I didn't need anyone.

I'd take care of myself.

Now and forever.

It was only me.

AIDEN
Then: Almost eight-years-old

I spent the rest of the night pretending like I wasn't there. Sitting in what Misty called "the common area" of the kid's shelter, I ignored everything around me as she did my paperwork.

"Here's your dinner," another woman said, placing a plate of food in my lap.

"I'm not hungry."

"Hey, everyone!" the same woman called out, not listening to me. Bringing the other kids' eyes over to us instead.

"Everyone say hello to Aiden Pierce. He's going to be staying here for a little while. I need everyone to make him feel welcome, alright?"

I went back to ignoring everything and everyone around me, staring at my plate of food. It didn't look like anything my mom ever made.

I don't know how much time went by before I heard, "So your name's Aiden?"

I looked up, seeing an older boy who was maybe twelve or thirteen-years-old standing there. Looking down at me like he had the right to.

"How old are you?"

I didn't answer him. All I wanted was to be left alone.

Why was that so hard for everyone to understand? Just leave me alone.

But he went on. "Why are you in foster care?"

I still didn't say a word, and I could tell by the look on his face, he was getting mad at me.

Screw him.

Screw all of them.

I hated this place.

I hated everything about this day, about this boy, about the kids around me.

I hated it all.

The boy didn't stop. He just stood taller, pushing his chest out in a big, bad, *I'm better than you,* sort of way.

"Don't you talk, or are you just stupid? Is that why you're here? Your mom didn't want to take care of her stupid son anymore?"

My teeth tightened, and my body shook, wanting to wipe that stupid smile off his face.

"Did your mom do drugs? Did she beat you? Why the fuck are you here, kid?"

An angry feeling deep in my stomach took over.

"I'm not looking for trouble. So back off," I told him.

"Oh... I know what happened now. Did she sell you?"

My heart started beating really fast, and my hands got really sweaty. I knew something bad was about to happen, and for the first time, I didn't care because all I wanted was my voice to be heard.

Someone, please ... just listen to me.

"You're a pretty fucking boy, so I bet she sold you. That's it, right? Did she sell you for drugs? Or did she sell you for dic—"

Before I knew what I was doing, I pushed my chair back and threw my plate of food in his face.

I didn't care he was bigger than me.

I didn't care that I was going to get in trouble.

I didn't care about anything other than shutting him up.

"What the fu—"

I ran my shoulder into his stomach as hard as I could, and he fell to the ground with me on top of him. The kids started hooting and hollering as we wrestled each other on the floor. It didn't surprise me that I could keep up with him, everyone always said I was big for my age.

"Break it up!" a man yelled from behind us, yanking me off the boy who looked like he was ready to kill me.

Yeah, me too, bro.

I shoved off the man I thought was the guard, and before anyone could say anything to me, I ran.

Except this time, it was straight toward the back door.

"Aiden, stop! Where are you going?" Misty yelled from somewhere in the room, but I ignored her too.

Taking off into the yard where there was a playground, going for the first hiding spot I could find.

Under the green slide.

Where I finally, for the first time that day...

Felt *safe*.

I let out a breath. The one I'd been holding from the second I walked into this stupid foster place. Wanting so badly to just run away.

Where would I go?

Who would I find?

What would happen to me?

Even though I wanted to be left alone, I hated that I was by myself. With no one to talk to, no one to make me feel like everything was going to be alright. I had nothing but the lonely, afraid feeling in my heart.

"Momma, why?" I quietly spoke out loud, hoping no one would hear me. "Why did you leave me all by myself? Who's going to protect me and love me? Who's going to be there for me? Who, Momma, who?"

"I'll share my dinner with you," someone offered out of nowhere in the sweetest voice I'd ever heard.

My eyes flew up, and I came face to face with a small, little girl with pretty, bright blue eyes standing over me. Holding onto her plate of food because it was the only thing she had to share, to give...

Me.

As if Momma had magically made her appear.

Did she?

"I don't like to be by myself either. It really sucks, but I can come under there with you, and then we can hide from the mean boy together."

I didn't know anything about girls, other than they whined and complained a lot. Especially the ones in my class at school. They were always telling on us.

"You're not going to tell Misty where I'm at?"

"Why would I do that?"

"Because you're a girl."

She looked at me like I was crazy. "Well, that's not my fault. I can't help that I'm a girl, God made me like this."

Maybe she wasn't a tattletale because Momma knew I didn't like tattlers, and she really did put her here for me. I guess that would make sense.

"I'm not hiding," I added, needing her to know.

I don't know why it bothered me, but I didn't want her to think I was a little boy.

I wasn't.

I'm a Little Man.

And for some reason, I just sat there and stared at her. My body starting to feel warm and funny with each minute that went by.

A smile appeared on her face, and it sparkled against the moon.

"It's okay to hide sometimes. I don't like Troy either, he's a bully and smells like a butthole. Donna is always yelling at him to go take a shower, saying he's never going to be adopted smelling like that, but who would want to adopt a bully butthole." She shrugged, and I busted out laughing.

I laughed so hard my head fell back, forgetting all about the lonely feeling in my chest.

"Well, aren't ya gonna ask me to sit down?" she let out, putting her head to the side. Placing her free hand on her hip.

Smiling wider.

I opened my mouth to reply, to say something, anything, but nothing came out. The only sound I made were these noises coming from the back of my throat I'd never made before.

She started giggling and wiggling and bouncing like she couldn't wait for me to answer. It was then I saw she was missing her two bottom teeth. She was so weird and pretty all at the same time. No, she wasn't pretty, she was beautiful. And she wasn't laughing but giggling.

Loudly.

The sound took over everything around us, making it impossible to ignore. It was so catchy that I started laughing too, and I had no idea what I was laughing about. Only that I had to laugh with her, making my stomach feel tight again.

"You're cute! I like you. Now scoot over for me."

I did, only because I liked the way she made me feel, and I didn't want her to leave me alone again. She sat right beside me as close as she could, leaving no room in between us.

"I'm Bailey Button, by the way."

Her soft skin brushed against my arm, causing new bubbles in my stomach.

What was that?

"I hate my name. It's so stupid. It sounds like I'm a belly button, but I'm not. I'm a girl, see?" Tugging on her hair that was in pigtails, she blinked her long, big eyelashes at me. "I don't look like a belly button, right?"

"No." Was the only word I could say when she sat that close to me.

She nodded, bringing a piece of chicken up to her mouth. Not paying any attention to what she was doing to me.

"I like your name, Aiden Pierce. It's pretty."

"Pretty?"

"Yeah, I like pretty names. Not like mine."

Before I gave it any thought, I blurted, "Your name is beautiful just like you are."

Her eyes flew to mine, and another huge smile took over her face. "No one has ever called me beautiful, Aiden Pierce!"

I smiled with her.

"Now we're going to have to get married."

"What?" I stopped smiling, jerking back. "We do?"

"Mmm hmm..." She chewed on her food, swallowing it down. "That's what happens when you call a girl beautiful, you have to get married after. I don't make the rules, I just follow them. Before my momma passed away, she always said to marry a man who calls me beautiful, and I'll be happy every day of my life."

Maybe her momma sent her to me too?

"Will you make me happy?"

"Uh... I can try."

"Try really hard, okay?"

"Okay."

Momma would want that, right?

Yeah, she would.

"I like the way Bailey Pierce sounds. What do you think?"

"I like the way Bailey Pierce sounds too, but aren't we too young to get married?"

"No silly! I meant when we're older."

"Oh." I thought about it for a second. "Like how much older?"

Now it was her turn to think about it for a second. "Like when we're eighteen. That's old enough."

"Okay."

"Aiden..." She giggled, twirling her hair in a big knot around her finger. "You have to ask me first."

"Oh, I do?" I scratched my head. "When?"

"When we're eighteen."

"Okay." I nodded, meaning it. "I'll ask you when we're eighteen."

"Okay." She nodded back. "I'll try to act surprised too. Ask me in a good way, alright? So I cry."

She was confusing, but in the best way possible. I'd say anything she wanted just to keep her by my side, so I'd always feel this way.

Safe.

I knew right then and there my momma had something to do with this. I didn't know how, but she kept her promise to me. This had to be the girl, I felt it in my bones.

"Why would I want to make you cry?"

"Because they're happy tears and crying with happy tears is like super romantic."

"Oh... Okay then. I'll ask you in a way that will make you cry happy tears."

"Okay good, but don't make me cry in any other way than happy tears. Ever. You promise?"

"I promise."

She leaned her head on my shoulder, whispering, "I trust you."

She did?

Good, because for a reason I didn't understand, I trusted her too.

But it was the smell of her strawberry hair that was doing all sorts of things to my body. I hoped she didn't notice, I didn't want to scare her away. Not when I'd just found her.

Or did she find me?

"Oh, Aiden!" She threw her arms around my neck and jumped into my lap, sending the plate of food flying. I hesitated until she added, "I'm so happy I found you! You're better than that stray cat I fed that keeps coming back! So much better! I don't have to feed anymore strays because now, I have you! Finally! I found you! I found my family like my mom said I would!"

I hugged her back, holding her as close as I could to my body. Her heartbeat next to mine would now be my favorite feeling in the whole world.

Today had been the worst day of my life but meeting her has turned it into one of the best.

Thank you, Momma.

"I promise you, Bailey Button. We won't ever be alone again."

And I meant it with my whole heart and soul. Even though I didn't know what that was, it still sounded like everything I ever wanted.

And that was good enough for me.

Four

Camila

Now

"Your resumé states you have experience with children but doesn't specify when or how many children were under your care," the young woman interviewing me questioned as she skimmed through the papers in front of her. Fixating her bright blue eyes on me, she added, "Can you clarify?"

"Yes, of course." I eagerly nodded, clearing my throat. "I have siblings. Lots of them. I can't remember a time where our home wasn't filled with kids. You'd think my parents didn't own a television or something." I nervously laughed at my own joke. "I swear my biological clock is ticking inside my mother's body. She loves kids now as much as she did back then. All she wants is a team of grandbabies. My father is the same."

The woman laughed, and her smile lit up her entire face. I had only just met her, but I swear I knew her from somewhere.

Where do I know you from?

"I take it you don't have kids?"

I shook my head. "No, I don't, but I love kids. Especially babies. There is nothing better than holding a little babe in your arms, snuggling them close to your heart. Don't get me started on their soft skin, cute feet, and baby smell."

"That's how they get you," she chuckled. "Then they start walking and talking, and it all goes downhill from there."

I scoffed out a giggle. "My siblings were definitely a handful. They still are."

41

"I bet it's nice to come from a big family, though. I was an only child, and I always wished I had the same luck as you. But now"— she leaned back into her chair, lovingly holding onto her growing belly through her white sundress— "I just keep getting knocked up with my own."

We laughed, easing into a comfortable conversation with one another like old friends. I liked her. She seemed genuine, and that was hard to find amongst women these days. Particularly the one I could possibly be working for.

"My husband is adamant about knocking me up with triplets."

"Three more babies? All at once? You must have the patience of a saint. I mean, you already have three kids—"

"No, no, no!" she chimed in, chuckling. "The nanny position you're interviewing for isn't for me."

"Oh… I thought… I just assumed … you're interviewing me, so I just… I mean … never mind." I shifted in the leather chair across from her, wringing my clammy hands together in my lap, trying to gather my composure.

My eyes glanced all around the room to look at anything besides her. It was only then I noticed a couple broken picture frames on the mantle in the office we sat in. Even though the glass was shattered, someone had set them back up.

What's that about?

I thought to myself, biting my tongue, struggling with my English like I always did when I was nervous.

"It's alright. That would have been my assumption as well. But no, I'm just a good friend of the family."

My mind immediately swarmed with an endless list of questions about said family.

Where were the parents?

Why aren't they here?

Will I be meeting them today?

However, I knew it wasn't my place to ask. I ignored each and every one of them, simply grateful that my uncle happened to overhear someone talking about hiring a full-time nanny.

My tio Feto said he had a family that he provided lawn service for, and they were looking to bring in help for their kids.

When he told me about the opening, it couldn't have come at a better time. Nursing school wasn't going to be cheap, and I needed a job to pay for my student loans that were already piling up. Working at my best friend Danté's club wasn't going to pay my bills or my student loans. I needed a real job.

Education was my only way out of living in Selma, otherwise known as *El Barrio*, the hood. I couldn't afford anywhere else and I wanted a better life for myself.

I spent two hours on the public transportation bus just to get to this interview, and already it felt like I was screwing it up.

"You have an accent. Where are you from?"

As much as I tried covering it up, I should have known it'd be useless. It didn't matter that I was bilingual, Spanish would always be my native tongue.

Pulling myself together, I didn't bother hiding my accent this time. Responding, "My siblings and I were born here, but my parents are from Venezuela. But it won't be a concern," I quickly vowed. "My English is perfect, except when I get nervous, my Spanish tends to come out. I'll speak English with the kids, that won't be a problem. I promise."

She narrowed her eyes at me. "Why would that be a problem?"

"Because it had been an issue all my life. I'd been treated like a minority ever since I could remember."

"Well that won't be a problem in this house."

Damn it, I just said that out loud.

I was never one to not speak my mind, often digging my own grave. I was opinionated, I couldn't help it. You try growing up in a house full of Venezuelan people. I spoke my mind loudly, or I wouldn't have been heard.

"They would love if their children learned another language. Aside from cusswords, you'd think their boys barely spoke English."

I relaxed, instantly at ease. Her confession had me wanting the position even more. Working for a family who treated me as an equal was something a girl like me only dreamt about. My family was poor, but they were hardworking.

We had what we needed growing up, food on the table, clothes on our backs, and a roof over our heads.

As if she could read my thoughts, her pointed stare never wavered from my eyes once.

"Why don't you tell me a little bit about yourself? Who is Camila Jiménez?"

Swallowing the lump that had formed in my throat, I countered, "What would you like to know? Skyler, right?" Silently hoping I remembered her name correctly from when she introduced herself.

She nodded. "Yes. Skyler Jameson, but you can call me Sky. Everyone besides my husband calls me that."

Her name even sounded familiar.

Where do I know you from? Just shut up and smile, Camila. Just shut up and smile.

"How about we start with how old you are?"

"I'm twenty-eight."

"Are you married? Single? Never dating again?"

I laughed. "I had a boyfriend once, and I learned quickly that guys kind of suck. Besides, I don't have any time for that. Between school, studying, work, and being there for my family when they need me, I barely have time to breathe." I shrugged, playing it off like it wasn't a big deal. It wasn't, at least not for me.

"My family is everything to me. I helped raise my siblings, always trying to set the best example for them. With some it worked, with others not so much. I may not have the work experience you're looking for on paper, but I know what to do when a baby is crying. I know kids can be a pain as much as they can be a blessing. But at the end of the day, all they need is love. The rest just kind of falls into place."

She beamed, smiling big and wide. The expression illuminating her face again. "How do you feel about overnight stays? I've been staying with the kids at night, but I will be needing a replacement soon."

The parents don't come home?

"That won't be a problem."

"How about cooking and cleaning?"

"I love to cook. It's one of my favorite things to do. Cleaning too. It actually relaxes me."

"Yeah, Bailey too."

"Bailey is the mom?"

"Mmm hmm."

"Will I be mee—"

Dismissing my question, she gazed down, shuffling through a manila file of papers. "In case of an emergency, are you CPR certified?"

"Certified, no. But I do know how to perform CPR if needed."

"No worries, it won't be a problem to get your certification. I'll have Aiden's RN get me the information."

"Aiden is—"

"Possibly your new boss," she interrupted, locking eyes with me. "Dr. Aiden Pierce."

That explains the huge house and expensive looking ... everything.

"He's the Chief of Surgery at Docher Memorial Hospital in Southport. It says here you're in nursing school? Aiden will love that."

"Yeah. I love helping people. It's just who I am."

From the look on Skyler's face, she liked me, and the emotion was very much mutual.

"How about we continue this interview while I show you around?"

"That'd be great." I stood, straightening my long, flowy skirt before grabbing my bag from the floor. Calmly trying to hide my excitement of possibly getting the job, as I followed close behind her. Listening intently, while my eyes wandered with each step I took around the massive estate. Taking it all in.

The home was a disaster.

Toys, video games, clothes, anything and everything was scattered all over the floors with no end in sight. Piles of laundry covered the couches, food, and God knows what else, laid freely on the kitchen counters and dining table as if it'd been sitting there for days. Layers upon layers of dust coated the furniture and baseboards like they hadn't been wiped down in ages.

My small rundown apartment may have been falling apart at the seams, but it was clean. There was no way I could live like this. How such a beautiful home that someone obviously worked so hard for and allowed it to go to shit was mind-blowing to me.

I couldn't believe my eyes, seeing a life I didn't know existed. But under all the clutter I could still picture the beauty this home once held.

Starting from the expensive looking red front door, to the white picket fence, and the sunflowers all around. To the inside of the home where there was a grand staircase, contemporary furniture, and gorgeous marble floors throughout. The entire floorplan was exquisite.

This home was breathtaking. Anyone could see that.

A lot of time and devotion was put into every detail, down to the accent pillows on the sofas, and the accessories, such as a simple candle that read *Home Sweet Home* on the coffee table. To the profound love I could physically feel through the walls. Though there was something else circulating through the air.

A void so crippling.

So consuming.

So real.

I felt it down to my bones, down to the core of my being. Causing shivers to stir on every inch of my skin, making the ends of my hair stand straight up.

What the hell was that?

"Please excuse the mess," Skyler remarked, bringing my attention to her. "It wasn't always like this."

What did she mean by that?

"Between the boys and the baby girl, things have been hectic to say the least. I'm pregnant, and there's only so much I can help with. That's why I'm interviewing candidates for a full-time nanny position and part-time housekeeper. The kids need it as much as this house does."

"I can see that."

"Aiden works a lot and Bailey… she's not here so…" She shook her head. "The family needs help."

"When is she coming back?"

She cleared her throat. "It's not my place to say anything about anything," she anxiously let out. "Just know you're needed here, desperately. But in the meantime, you'll deal directly with me. At least for now."

"Does that mean I—" A shiny frame caught my attention from the corner of my eye, and I was suddenly stepping over a pile of Legos and cars to get to the main living room.

The family photos on the far wall immediately captured my stare, and my feet moved on their own accord. It was like this gravitational pull was dragging me toward the happy memories proudly displayed for all to see.

Glowing.

Radiating.

Exuding a happy, carefree family.

The man who I assumed was Dr. Pierce was probably somewhere in his mid-forties. His tan skin, long slender nose, and square jawline were as prominent as his crystal blue eyes. He had a graying five o'clock shadow and short brown, wavy hair that was also graying at his temples.

In the photos he was smiling in, it was his dimples that my eyes seemed to focus on the most. They made him appear younger, contrary to the tiny wrinkles in the corners of his eyes that gave away his age.

When my stare settled on the three cross tattoos on his neck, I recognized them instantly. Being raised in a religious family made me acknowledge the significance behind his black ink.

Representing the Father, the Son, and the Holy Spirit.

He was the first doctor I'd ever seen with tattoos visibly on display as if he wore them with honor. Someone doesn't just get a religious tattoo for shits and giggles, it meant something to him. Something deeper on a personal level.

Something that once again had me feeling some kind of way about a man I'd never met. Yet felt connected to in some way.

What the hell, Camila? He's your boss. Your married boss.

As if on cue, my gaze shifted toward his wife who was absolutely breathtaking. Her blue eyes sparkled against the lighting of the bright room. Only illuminating her contagious smile and petite features as her brown hair flowed through the wind in the photo.

She was a beauty.

A flawless beauty.

But it wasn't until I saw their wedding photo, that I let out the breath I didn't realize I was holding.

They were no doubt a stunning couple, and from the looks of it, very much in love. The devotion to their family emitted off every photo, causing me to smile as much as they were in the pictures. They looked like the perfect family, something you would see in catalogs and magazines. Without a care in the world.

"They were married young," Skyler shared, standing behind me. Noticing what photo my eyes were fixated on the most.

"I'm sorry." I spun, looking at her, blushing. "I didn't mean to stare."

"Trust me, it's hard not to stare. I remember the first time I met Aiden. I think I stared at his piercing blue eyes and dimples the entire time he was talking to me. He's always been easy on the eyes. You'd have to be blind to not be attracted to him. And don't get me started on Bailey, she's like a living, breathing *beauty*."

"That's exactly how I just thought of her."

"She looks like Belle from Beauty and the Beast, right?"

"Yes! That's what—"

"Everyone says. The first time they took the kids to Disney, they actually had children asking her if she was the real Belle. Aiden calls her Beauty because of it. It's been their thing since they were young."

"So, they've known each other for a long time."

She nodded. "A very long time."

"I can't wait to meet them. I mean … that's if I get the job."

"I would lo—"

A baby's wails echoed through the halls and off the monitor in her hand, interrupting us.

Skyler smirked, and with loving eyes she peered down the corridor where the cries were coming from.

Announcing, "Get ready to meet the sassiest baby girl in the world." Without saying another word, she nodded toward the room at the end of the hall and started walking as I followed behind her.

Moments later, she opened the door to the pair of bright blue eyes I had only just seen in photos.

Making me fall in love…
Instantaneously.

Five

Camila

Now

"Meet Journey Pierce," Skyler announced, picking the baby girl up from her crib and nestling her tiny frame against her chest. "Shhh … it's alright, Journey, it's okay…" she cooed, bouncing her in her arms as she made her way over to the changing table. "Are you wet? Huh? Is that why the world is ending?" She continued trying to calm her down while changing her diaper, but Little Miss wasn't having it.

She fell into a fit of rage as soon as the cold wet wipe hit her bottom, causing her pretty face to turn bright red as she made her presence known.

"She gets like this sometimes, and there's no calming her down, until she passes out from the exhaustion of her own meltdown." She buttoned up her onesie and straightened her outfit before picking her up again. "The doctor says it's normal, though, like anything else, it's just a phase that will pass. She's only six months old, but it still hasn't passed," Skyler shared over Journey's tantrum while she rocked her in her arms.

"I guess it's pretty handy to have a doctor in the house, huh?"

"Oh … no." She shook her head. "Aiden … he's … I mean he's not her doctor. He hasn't even held—"

BANG!

A door slammed shut from somewhere within the house, startling us both. Interrupting Skyler and making Little Miss even more pissed off.

What was she going to say?

49

He hasn't held what? His own daughter?

"That must be Jackson and Jagger. Is it three-thirty already?"

Looking at the time on my phone, I nodded.

"Do you mind holding her for a few minutes, while I go take care of the boys?"

"Not at all." I smiled, wanting to hold Journey from the moment I saw her. "Are Jackson and Jagger their sons?"

"Yes. Just wait, they're more of a handful than this one." She nervously chuckled, carefully handing the baby off to me. "Well, Jackson more than Jagger. You'll see soon enough."

I cradled Journey in my arms, positioning her flailing body next to my heart. There was something about the rhythmic beating that reminded babies of their time in the womb. It used to work for my siblings whenever they were losing it.

"How old are they?"

"Jackson is going to be thirteen, and Jagger is going to be eleven."

"Wow. That's quite the age gap between them and her."

"Yeah." She cautiously nodded with an expression on her face I couldn't quite read. "They tried a long time for Journey. She was so loved and wanted before she was even born. They all were, but she was on a whole different level. Especially for Aiden."

I wanted to ask why the sudden sadness in her tone, when she was talking about such a beautiful creation. A baby girl who was obviously made from so much love.

It almost seemed as though everything Skyler had shared up until that point was laced with heartache and sorrow.

But why?

What happened?

Nothing made sense, and the more I tried to analyze the situation, the more I came up empty. These emotions were playing with my mind, and they were starting to give me whiplash. There was already this gravitational pull toward a family I hadn't even met but felt a profound connection to.

"I'll be right back," Skyler stated, reverting my attention to the screaming baby in my arms.

"No worries, I got her. By all means, take your time."

She gave us one last look before she turned and left the room. Slightly shutting the door behind her, leaving baby girl and me alone.

"Alright, Little Miss, no need to show off. I get it, you're here, and you're fierce and mighty," I coaxed, gazing down at her adoringly. Immediately noticing how much she resembled her mother. "You are a beauty, Journey. Do you have any idea how beautiful you are? Even with all this crying and all those tears, you're still a stunning baby."

Her wails started getting louder and louder, rumbling out of her full force. If she didn't stop soon, she was going to make herself sick.

"Alright, that's enough of that ... come on ... you can do it... I know you can do it," I soothed in a lulling tone, grabbing an old, worn down Ninja Turtle blanket from her crib. "You're a girl. Why do you have a boy blanket? Hmm ... maybe I'll bring you back a new, soft, pink blanket if I get the job of taking care of you, Journey. What do you think? You like that idea?"

"Wahhhhh!"

"Okay, never mind. Ninja Turtle blanket it is." Even though she was a little too old to be swaddled, I did it anyway. Seeing if maybe that would help.

It didn't.

Her ear-piercing screams could wake up the dead.

"Phew ... you got a set of lungs on ya, kid." I moved around the vast room which was more like a suite than a nursery, still rocking and bouncing her.

My eyes scanned the space, noticing for the first time her room was something out of a magazine as well. The walls were a pale pink with white crown molding. The furniture looked vintage and expensive. Her crib was decked out in whites, grays, and pinks with Journey written in script on the wall.

The space was gorgeous. Black and white portraits lined the walls with two large book cases, and an old wooden rocking chair that had intricate designs on the back were situated in the corner by the bay window.

"Shhh, shhh, shhh. Look at all these books, Journey. Shhh, shhh, shhh. How about we try to read one?"

As if she understood what I was asking, she sucked back another sob.

"Okay, we're onto something. What do you want to read? Hmm? Let's see what we got." I grabbed the furthest one in the corner. "Baby Einstein?"

"Wahhhh!"

"Definitely not that one." I grabbed the one on the other end. "Goodnight Moon?"

"Wahhhh! Wahhhh! Wahhhh!"

"Alright, you definitely don't like that one."

Reaching for the book in the middle of her collection, my eyes caught a story hiding behind all the other books instead.

I gasped, "Little Miss, look what I found. This is my favorite book of all time. It looks like it might be yours too. Hmmm ... is that why it looks like it's been read hundreds of times? Is *On the Night You Were Born* your favorite too?"

She whimpered, sniffling.

"Ah, good choice."

I sat in the rocking chair in the corner of the room, reading her the story, and with each turn of the page she cried a little less. Until finally...

She was calm.

Listening intently to every word that fell from my lips. Softly smiling and showing off the two tiny teeth she was cutting on the bottom.

Of course, that explained a lot. She was teething.

I didn't have to spend hours with Journey to know that this baby girl would own my heart and soul.

I grinned, rubbing her soft cheek with the back of my hand. "Are we friends now?"

She cooed, kicking her chubby, little legs at me.

Smiling.

Drooling.

Squirming.

Being the most adorable thing I'd ever seen.

"Now what? What do you want to do? Should we go look for Skyler?"

"Wah!"

"Alright, alright, we don't have to go look for her. I don't want to share you anyway."

She cooed again, and I swear she understood me. Already, we had this crazy bond, and I'd only been with her for maybe twenty minutes.

"You want to sing? How about we sing?"

She wiggled and giggled and drooled some more. Gnawing on her little fingers to sooth her gums.

"What should we sing? Oh! I know. How about this? *The sun'll come out tomorrow, bet all those dollars that tomorrow. There'll be sun shining bright and happiness. Just thinkin' about tomorrow.*"

Her face lit up, and her eyes widened, kicking harder and faster than she was before.

"Oh, you like *Annie*, do you? *Just thinkin' about tomorrow. Clears away the sadness, the rain, and the empti—*"

"Oh my God, Sky! Just back off! We don't want or need you here! Go home and raise your own damn kids!"

"Jackson! Don't you walk away from me! You come back here right now!"

"Screw you, Sky! I'm so sick of your shit!"

I jerked back from hearing the disrespect spewing out of this boy's mouth from the hallway.

"You're just as big of a pain in the ass as your niece! But at least I can make Harley go away! Wish I could say the same for you!"

"Jackson! I get it! You're angry! We're all angry! Do you think this is easy on any of us?"

"You don't know anything! Especially, how I'm feeling!"

"Jackson, I'm just trying to help!"

"Nobody wants your help! When are you gonna get that?"

"You need my help, your dad needs—"

"My dad?" he scoffed out with pure disgust I could feel through the walls. "You're seriously going to play that card? Oh, come on, Sky! That's a joke, and you know it!"

"That's not fair. Your dad needs you now more than ever, and you being a little shit doesn't help any!"

"Where's my dad, Sky?! Huh? Tell me! Where's the man who needs me! Because I haven't seen him in months! But why would he come home when you're always here taking care of his responsibilities!"

I should've stayed out of it.

It was none of my business.

I should've stopped myself from walking toward that door...

From standing in that hallway...

From opening my mouth when he shouted, "How many times do I have to tell you, you're not my mother?! So just turn your ass around and go home for once! Nobody wants you here!"

"Jackson Pierce, you do not talk to her that way!"

Instantly, everyone's heated glares shifted toward me. My eyes widening when I realized what I had just done.

Jackson narrowed his eyes at me, scanning me up and down with a demeaning stare. "Who the hell are you?"

"Jackson," Skyler snarled, bringing his attention back to her. "I'm interviewing her to possibly be your new nanny."

His mouth dropped open, snapping, "Are you fuc—"

"Boy, you finish that sentence, and I swear I will wash your mouth out with soap. Do you understand me?" I warned, interrupting him.

"Oh ... this is bulls—"

The expression on my face was enough to render him silent.

He scowled, shaking his head as he backed away. "Whatever." Eyeing only me. "At least Mary Poppins is hot. Maybe her ass will make my dad leave the hospital and come home for once."

I jerked back, and Skyler seethed, "Jackson Pierce! You apologize! Right now!"

He rolled his eyes, snidely smiling. "You're the one who hired her, right?" He shrugged. "Should have thought of that before you decided we needed a babysitter. I am a growing boy, after all. So now what? Should we call you Mommy?"

"Oh my God, Jackson," she bellowed, her face turning bright red from embarrassment.

Mirroring mine, I was sure.

Before either of us could say another word, he abruptly spun around and stomped into what I assumed was his bedroom. Slamming the door so hard behind him, it vibrated the walls down the long hall.

Skyler sighed deeply with humiliation clearly written across her face. "Wow ... that is not how I thought this would go down. I'm so sorry, Camila. I completely understand if you no longer want the position. I truly apologize for wasting your time." She spun and walked away. "I'll see you out."

I peered from her, to Jackson's door, to the other boy Jagger, who I'd just noticed was standing behind the wall where Skyler was arguing with Jackson. His face looked as thrown off by the whole encounter as we were.

Both sons were spitting images of their father with brown hair and piercing blue eyes.

"I have to ask," Skyler stated, interrupting my train of thought. Once again staring at me. "That song ... the song you were singing to Journey. Why that song?"

"The *Annie* song?" I replied, caught off guard. Realizing she was still holding the baby monitor in her hand.

"Yeah. Out of all the songs you could sing to her, why that one?"

"Oh ... um... I used to sing it to my siblings all the time. They loved it. I mean, my sisters must have watched the original movie a thousand times."

"You never saw the remake?"

"No. Why?"

"You really don't know who I am, do you, Camila?"

I arched an eyebrow, taking her in from her head to her toes. "I'm sorry, I don't know—"

"Please don't apologize. When I first promised Bailey I'd be here for her family, I was terrified I wouldn't find the right woman to help me take this on. I had this nagging fear the women I interviewed would be here for the wrong reasons. For who I am and not for the kids. I didn't want to mess it up, you know?"

I nodded, perceiving she was trying to tell me something deeper and more meaningful.

"Bailey's my best friend. She's the older sister I always wanted. When we first met, she didn't know who I was either, and because of that I loved her instantly. To go from my world, to one where no one knows who I am, was something I prayed for every night. I used to be a celebrity, an actress, and singer. It was a hard life, and if you Googled my name you'd know why. So, to finally find that in her...

well, it meant… everything. I guess I'm just trying to say that," she breathed out, shaking her head. "I don't know what I'm trying to say."

I didn't hesitate in replying, "Like me being here is meant to be."

"Yeah, but that's crazy, right?"

I was the first to break our intense stare, gazing down at the sleeping baby girl who wasn't fazed in the slightest by what just occurred.

As if I brought her the peace she'd been fighting for.

"No. I don't think that's crazy at all."

She scoffed out a smile, about to turn back around.

This unexplainable sentiment took over every inch of my body. I couldn't ignore it.

I was there for a reason, and without thinking twice about it, I asked, "When can I start?"

Knowing in my heart…

This was where…

I   was   supposed   to   be.

Six

Camila

Now

To say I wasn't nervous for my first day at the Pierce residence couldn't be further from the truth. I was beyond anxious for what would happen once I stepped foot into their house again tomorrow morning. Hoping, praying I would be accepted, but knowing deep down there was no way in hell it would be that easy.

At least not so soon.

The crazy thing was, as nervous as I felt, it didn't overpower the fact that I was also very much excited. I wanted to help this family as best as I could, fully aware it wasn't going to be a walk in the park.

If anything, it was going to be a lot harder than I imagined it would be. I was up for the challenge, though. There wasn't much that scared me in life, but with that being said, letting someone down who counted on me was one of the things I feared the most. And it wasn't just Skyler who was relying on me, it was the entire family.

They just didn't know it yet.

My cell phone ringing on my coffee table tore me away from my trancelike state, only thinking about the Pierces. I hadn't stopped thinking about them since I left their home almost three days ago.

The events played over in my head.

My encounter with the oldest boy, Jackson, the Little Miss Journey in my arms, the pictures, the house, it all replayed on a constant loop in my head. There were so many unanswered questions that had no rhyme or reason. They were just there, lurking in the forefront of my mind.

Waiting...

For I don't know what.

"Jesus, Camila, stop," I ordered myself, reaching for my phone from the couch. "Hello," I answered, shaking away the uncertainty that was starting to take its toll on me.

"Camila, mami! Que paso, chica? Donde tu andas?" Danté asked, shouting over the loud Reggaetón music blaring in the background. *"What's up, girl? Where you at?"*

"I'm home."

"Perro, chica, te necesito para ahora," he added, *"But, girl, I need you tonight."*

"Danté, I already told you. I got a job. A *real* job, and I start tomorrow. I'm not working at your club tonight."

"Camila, mamita, you break my heart. You're my girl. I need you."

"You're going to have to find a new girl."

"Sean know you got a new gig?"

I rolled my eyes. "Sean doesn't run my life, Danté."

"He know that?"

"I'm hanging up now."

"Wait, wait, wait... Listen, I need ya. I'm down a bartender. Come on, do it for me. We go way back, Camila. I need you. You owe me."

I rolled my eyes again. "How many times are you going to play the 'You owe me' card, Danté?"

"As many times as it takes. Mira, mamita, I know you're smilin' behind that bitchy face you got goin' on these days. 'Cuz I know my girl Camila loves to dance, and I know you hear that Reggaetón music bumpin' behind me. Gurl, stop playin'. Come shake dem sexy ass hips over here for me tonight."

I broke out laughing, I couldn't help it. Danté had that pull about him, he could make a dying man laugh his ass off.

"The Sean bullshit aside, mamita, you were my girl before his. Ya tu sabes," he reminded, *"You know that."*

"Sean around?" I questioned, needing to know what I was getting myself into.

Danté I could handle, Sean was a different story. An extremely different story. I wasn't lying when I told Skyler I had a boyfriend once.

I did.

It just happened to be the same guy I dated more than once...

"You know him, Camila, he always be somewhere. You got into that fancy nursin' school, you gotta pay those student loans somehow, don't ya, mamita? And I pay you cash, under the table cash. So be the good girl we both know you are and help a brotha' out. I need you. Nobody needs you like me, Camila."

"Is this you trying to sweet talk me?"

"Depends. Is it workin'? Or do I need to play the best friend card too?"

He was right, I had loans piling up a mile a minute. Besides, the club was within walking distance of my apartment, and maybe it would help take my mind off the Pierces. At least for the rest of the night. Between school and working at Danté's club, I never needed more than two to three hours of sleep anyway. My body was used to it.

"Fine," I muttered, standing up to walk over to my closet at the far corner of my small studio apartment. "Throw in two hundred dollars on top of what you tip me out tonight, and I'll be there with bells on." I smiled, even though he couldn't see me.

"Ah! You be wheelin' and dealin' me. Alright, alright, I see you. Two hundred on top of tip out. Cash. Just how you like it. No bells needed, just go throw on a tight little mini, and I'll see you in an hour."

He hung up before I could change my mind, knowing he had me right where he wanted me. Waiting hand and foot on the guests at his club, wearing a short dress with my boobs hanging out. But just to be a rebel, I dressed in a tight pair of dark low-rise blue jeans that hugged my curves in all the right places with a white cotton shirt I cut into a crop top that read 'Sassy' across my breasts.

My long, wavy brown hair accentuated the words, drawing more attention to my cleavage on full display. I didn't have a huge rack by any means, but I knew how to work with what I did have. A push-up bra was my best friend on nights like this.

The more I showed, the more tips I made.

Although I had a petite frame, my narrow waist made my hips look curvier than they actually were. Emphasizing my plump, round booty. I added a pair of red hooker heels to complete my outfit.

Standing, I looked myself over in the full-length mirror. Fluffing my boobs a little more, giving the girls one last shake before I walked into my bathroom to do my makeup.

What would I do if I saw Sean tonight?

I hadn't seen him in a few weeks, and in Sean's world, that meant years. He used to flip his shit if he didn't see me at least once a day, having to keep tabs on me everywhere I went. To say he was controlling would be an understatement, but I guess that's what happens when you grow up together.

We were getting into trouble before we even knew the meaning of the word. It didn't help we grew up in a shady ass neighborhood where everyone was a two-bit hustler in some way, shape, or form.

Skyler didn't need to know all of that, she wouldn't have understood even if I told her. No one would, unless they grew up where we did. It was why I wanted a better life for myself. I deserved it.

Sean never understood what I wanted, always thinking he was already giving me the life I dreamed of. Wheeling and dealing in everything and anything he could get his hands on.

Trust me, it was never a good sign when people were scared of your boyfriend.

I was never scared of him. I'd known him all my life. We went from being friends to being in a relationship really young and at that time, I didn't know what I wanted out of a man. Sean definitely wasn't it, and it took me years to figure that out.

In his eyes, I would be his forever.

"Camila, how do you get yourself into these situations?" I asked my reflection in the bathroom mirror, shaking my head.

Quickly shifting gears, I thought about the makeup I was going to wear instead. To make my dark, almond-shaped eyes pop I drew on a wing liner. Lining the bottom of my eyes as well. Coating my long, thick lashes in mascara next, it gave me the sultry appearance I wanted.

Finishing off my look, I contoured my slender nose, high-rounded cheekbones and forehead, and added some bronzer to accentuate my already tan skin. Deciding at the last second to use a nude shade of gloss on my full, pouty lips. I smacked my pout together, smiling once I was done.

Getting tips had never been a problem for me. I was a pretty girl, and I used it to my advantage like any other good bartender would do. I'd been working at Danté's club on and off ever since he opened the place six years ago, but I'd decided it'd be best to keep it off my résumé.

Too many questions would arise that I didn't want to answer.

First and foremost, how I got paid.

I grabbed a bottled water from the fridge and locked up my apartment. Nodding to the Little Man who was playing with his firetrucks outside his door in our hallway, while his mom tended to her "guests" inside, waiting for it to be over.

"You watch my place, alright? Make sure no one tries to break in," I told him, smirking.

"I got you, Camila," Curtis replied with the swagger of a man, when he was only nine-years-old.

I hid back a laugh.

He hit on me like always, babbling, "I got some new hotrods in my house if you want to check them out when you get back." Already acting like he was grown.

"Curtis! How many times do I have to tell you? I'll be an old lady by the time you're my age."

"So … you ain't an old lady now."

"And you're only nine."

"Age is just a number."

I laughed, rustling up his dreads as I made my way down the stairs.

"Be good, Little Man! Use the key to my place if you need it!"

"Thanks, Camila! Go make that money, baby!"

"Curtis!"

"Yeah, whatever," he grumbled, making me chuckle again.

As soon as I stepped out in front of my complex, I ignored the hooting and hollering and the intense stares of the men standing outside. Ogling me like I was theirs to gawk at.

I bit my tongue, wanting to give them a piece of my mind, but ultimately, I chose to keep my mouth shut. In the long run, it would only get me in trouble, and the last thing I needed was for Sean to find out about it and be the reason for bloodshed.

For them.

It didn't take long for me to get to the club, walking in at the exact moment the beat was going off. The D.J. was dropping loud and fast, causing heads and bodies to shake every which way all around me. Making my hips sway to the Reggaetón music as I shuffled through the mass of people who were there to have a damn good time.

Knowing Danté would provide exactly that.

"Camila!" he shouted, lifting the hinged section of the counter up so I could walk behind the bar. "Ah, shit! I see you, mamita! Take it down! Hands on your knees! Show me what'cha workin' wit'!"

And I did.

Dropping it low to the ground in front of him, only to slowly roll my hips back up to grind right against him.

"There's my girl," he whispered into my ear, rocking his hips to the same rhythm as mine.

It was harmless fun. Danté was my oldest and dearest friend, and he also went to bat for the same team, not that it mattered to me. Men flocked to him like bees to honey. He was thin but built, had flawless cocoa skin, and a pretty boy face with his big honey-colored eyes that had lashes for days.

Always wearing the new fashion in clothes, shoes, accessories. He reminded me a lot of Lafayette in *True Blood*, looked a lot like him as well.

I was proud as hell of him for the success of his club. It may have been in the shitty part of town, but this was always the place to be on any given night.

"I knew you couldn't stay away," he teased, turning me toward the bar to get to work.

And once again, I did.

Loving every second of the tunes blaring from the speakers, and the energy of the crowd losing their minds.

"I'll take a Corona!"

"A rum and Coke!"

"I'm getting married this weekend! Woooohoooo! I'll take a round of shots for my girls and me!"

"Patron on ice!"

I listened to every order coming in from my section of the bar, nodding and making eye contact so they'd know I heard them, and they wouldn't try to order from someone else.

Round after round, I laid out drink orders in front of my customers. Never stopping to rest for even a second during my shift, taking orders as swiftly as my body moved to the sound of the music. Finding my steady pace.

I was Danté's girl for a reason, being the best bartender this place had ever seen won me that title.

Minutes turned into hours, and right when I thought I'd made it through a night at the club without seeing the man who claimed I was his queen, I felt *him* before I saw him.

Gazing straight up through the crowd of people, our eyes locked as if he could feel me too. There Sean was, all six-feet-four inches of him, wearing baggy jeans that hung off his waist with a black button-down shirt that I just knew was concealing his Glock. The one of many he didn't have a license for. Sean was always packing, and I wasn't just referring to the gun tucked in the back of his jeans.

But it wasn't until the smell of his tight leather jacket that hugged his bulky, muscular build, along with the spicy scent of his cologne I'd been buying him since we were kids assaulted my senses, did my heart skip a beat.

Our sexual attraction to each other had never been our problem. It was the fact that he couldn't keep his eyes, hands, or dick solely for me.

Except, you wouldn't think that by the way he was undressing me with his eyes, making his way over. Looking like trouble with a capital T with that certain swagger only Sean could exude. He caught the attention of every woman in the bar, and he knew it too.

It was his mutt genes that made him stand out the most. He was a mix of white, black, and Hispanic. Giving him light brown skin and entrancing green eyes that I swear could see into my soul. And because of that, I was the first to break our connection, pretending as if this didn't just happen.

I continued to take orders and went back to bartending. Acting as if he didn't exist, and he wasn't just there…

For me.

"Hey, baby," he greeted at the side of my face, getting as close to me as possible. "Where ya been, suga'?"

"That will be forty bucks," I addressed the man ordering drinks in front of me, focusing on him.

Disregarding my rapidly beating heart.

Stupid heart.

Sean questioned, "This how you gonna play it, baby?" Leaning closer to my neck, he faintly skimmed his soft lips against my pulse. "Don't try me, Camila, 'cuz I'll show you how many fucks I give. I won't be ignored."

Snatching the money out of my customer's hand, I abruptly turned toward the cash register. Only to be brought closer to the son of a bitch baiting me.

"Last warnin', baby."

I snapped my eyes to his, spewing, "I didn't hear the first one."

He grinned, narrowing his eyes at me with a predatory regard that made my thighs clench. "Even when you hate me, Camila, you know you still love me. So why don't ya bring those dick-suckin' lips over to me, and I'll remind you what to do with that mouth."

"You wanna piece of me, Sean?" I asked, cocking my head to the side. "That what you want?"

"Always. I'll fuck the bitch right outta you. You know you're my queen. I know you miss me, baby. Now let me take care of you, ya don't need to be workin' for some fuckin' doctor. I'll give you babies if that's what ya want. You don't need to be raisin' someone else's when you could be raisin' ours."

It didn't surprise me in the least he knew about the Pierces. Sean knew everything. Especially when it came to me.

"Awe, Sean," I voiced with nothing but sarcasm in my tone. "You just made my day."

He eyed me up and down, licking his lips. "I'll make your night too."

"You know what, just for that." Topping off a glass of whiskey, his favorite. I stated, "You should cool off."

Before he realized what I was about to do, I threw the drink in his face. Right into his eyes.

"You fuckin' bitc—"

"Oh, I'm sorry, Sean. This is how many fucks I give, *baby*."

With that, I turned around and left him there. Letting the groupies of women he ran around on me with tend to his burning eyes.

Giving, zero fucks...

About what I just did.

Seven

Camila

Now

The sound of the alarm on my phone woke me up bright and early.

Way too bright and early if you asked me.

No matter what time I fell asleep, six a.m. always came far too quickly. The sun was barely peeking through the vertical blinds in my studio apartment when my eyes finally started fluttering open.

"Uhhh…" I groaned, trying to find the button to shut off my alarm.

I didn't get home last night, or should I say this morning, 'til a little after four a.m., but who's to say what time I actually found sleep.

"Alright, Camila, get up," I ordered myself, shaking off the tiredness I still felt.

The smell of coffee brewing in the air was the real reason my ass got out of bed. Thanking God I remembered to set it to automatic brew, needing the caffeine in my veins. Though it was the music on my phone I turned on before I jumped in the shower that really started waking me up. The beat to "7 Rings" by Ariana Grande blared through the speakers as I washed my face.

Singing, *"Been through some bad shit I should be a savage, who would have thought it turned me into a savage."*

Using my shampoo bottle as a microphone, I broke it down. The girl spoke to my soul. I danced around, singing as loud as I could while I washed my hair and body.

"I bought a crib just for the closet."

By the time Ariana and I were wrapping up our number one hit, my shower was over.

"That's right, girl, one day I'm going to want it and get it too," I laughed, drying myself off. Thinking about how much money I'd be making once I was a registered nurse.

I went about my normal morning routine, deciding to dress in some skinny jeans with holes in them and a white cotton t-shirt I tucked into the side of my pants. Giving me that comfortable put together look I always wore. I'd be hanging with Little Miss most of the day, so being comfy was key.

I left my hair to dry naturally curly and just sprayed some product in it to control the frizz, or else I'd end up looking like a French poodle.

There wasn't much I did to my face, except add a little concealer under my eyes and some mascara to my lashes to appear more awake. At the last minute I decided to apply a bit of blush and gloss on my lips, and I was out the door with a bagel in one hand and a coffee in the other.

Making sure to grab an extra bagel for Little Man who I knew would be waiting outside his door for his breakfast. We'd made it a habit of walking to the bus stop together, his for school and mine for wherever I was headed that day. Public transportation was a way of life for me. I didn't own a car, I couldn't afford one.

Today, it was the Pierces.

My first day of working for them.

"Hey, baby," Curtis greeted, leaning against his door with his arms folded over his chest. The same shit-eating smirk appearing on his face.

I rolled my eyes, ignoring him. "Curtis, did you study for your math test?"

"Ugh, why you always gotta start the mornins' off with askin' me 'bout school?"

"Because someone has to," I reminded, handing him his bagel.

"Did you use the cream cheese I like?"

I arched an eyebrow, waiting.

"I mean, thank you."

"Yes. I used the cream cheese you like." Nodding to the stairs in front of us, I ruffled his dreads. "Come on or you're going to be late."

"Camila, I don't wanna go to school," he whined as we made our way down the stairs.

This was the biggest problem in our neighborhood. Parents making babies when they had no right to. They could barely take care of themselves, let alone the kids they were popping out left and right. Not giving them any encouragement to want to do something better with their lives.

"Then who's going to take care of me when I'm old if you don't get an education?"

"There are other ways of makin' money other than school, Camila."

"Is that right?"

"Yeah. Andre says I could join his crew—"

"Curtis! How many times have I told you to stay away from Andre? You know he's up to no good. You want to end up in juvie like he has *dozens* of times?"

He bowed his head. "No, ma'am."

"Oh, now I'm 'ma'am'?"

"I don't like it when my girl's mad at me."

"Curtis, I'm not your girl."

"Right." Thinking about it for a second, he looked up at me with a toothy grin. Adamantly responding, "You're my woman."

Trying to hide back a laugh, I choked on my coffee instead.

This kid...

"I'll tell you what ... you go to school all week without complaining about it, and I'll take you out for your favorite ice cream this weekend."

If there was one thing I learned about kids throughout the years, it was if all else failed...

Bribe them.

"Throw in a cream soda and a cookie, and you got yourself a deal," he negotiated, stopping in front of his school bus.

"Alright, Little Man, you drive a hard bargain, but you got yourself a deal." I extended out my fist. "Knuckles."

"Knuckles," he repeated, bumping his fist into mine.

"Be good in school, okay? And really try on your math test, don't just fill in the questions with random answers."

"Yeah, yeah, yeah." He smiled, stepping onto the bus.

I waited until his bus driver drove away before walking a couple streets over to my stop. I needed to make sure he didn't play hooky once he couldn't see me anymore.

"Hey, Camila," Deborah, the driver announced as I stepped on. "Start that new job today?"

"I do."

"You'll do amazing, you're great with kids. They're lucky to have you."

"Thanks for the reassurance."

"How's the daddy look?"

"Deborah," I chuckled, shaking my head.

"What, girl? You can look, just don't touch. And if you touch, don't get caught."

"Oh my God! You're horrible. He's my boss."

"That's how you get a raise."

I laughed, shaking my head again. Parking it right in my usual seat up front, closest to the door. I'd taken the bus enough times to avoid getting stuck in the back, where people took their sweet ass time getting off.

Swinging my bag on my lap, I pulled out my headphones and listened to my bus playlist for the entire two-hour ride to the Pierce residence. Thanking God the bus stop was only a ten-minute walk to their home.

My feet were killing me from last night, but I had zero regrets about working late. On top of the two-hundred we agreed to, Danté tipped me out another three hundred bucks. I made five hundred dollars in the matter of a few hours.

Nothing paid like bartending did, and I was slowly realizing I might be okay after all. It wouldn't be the first time I held two jobs down, sometimes I even held down three. I still helped my parents with some of their bills, even though I didn't live there anymore. And there was always a sibling asking me for money, which I never said no to.

I was a sucker, and they knew it.

"See ya later, Deborah." I waved goodbye and jumped off the bus, taking a deep breath as she drove away.

I wasn't due at the Pierces until nine, but I always made it a point to arrive early anywhere I went. Skyler was meeting me at their home this morning and it made me a little less nervous about what I would be walking into.

A little.

The nerves were still very much alive and present as I knocked on their door.

"Come in!" Skyler shouted from inside.

I inhaled yet another deep breath, blowing it out slowly. Trying the best I could to gather my composure as I turned the knob and opened the door.

"You got here just in time," Skyler stressed, looking as exhausted as I felt with a fidgety Journey in her arms.

Reassuring me of one thing and one thing only, this wasn't going to be easy. The boys must have put her through the ringer for hiring me in the first place. That also meant….

War.

With me.

To both of our surprise, Little Miss reached for me. And I'm not talking about a reflex move, where she just wanted out of the arms of the woman who was obviously frazzled, but truly went for me. Recognizing me immediately.

Arms.

Body.

Legs.

She pretty much catapulted herself into my arms, where I had no choice or say but to hold her. Like a stage five clinger.

"Wow!" Skyler marveled with the same stunned expression as me. "She's never done that before, with anyone. Even me. And I'm around her all the time."

I shrugged it off, not wanting to make a big deal out of it and hurt Skyler's feelings. It was evident she loved Journey and was caught off guard by her choosing me over her.

"Babies don't know what they want," I reasoned while Journey made herself at home in my arms.

As if she understood Skyler and wanted to prove her right, she laid her head on my shoulder, smiled, and then stuck her thumb in her mouth. Glaring at her like she was the enemy who had been keeping her away from me these last few days.

I nervously chuckled, this wasn't starting off how I'd hoped.

Please don't fire me because the baby wants me more than you...

People were funny like that, thinking they wanted a nanny until they realized they could be replaced. I didn't know Skyler well enough to know how she'd react.

However, I'd be lying if I said I wasn't shocked when she smiled lovingly at us and breathed out a huge sigh of relief.

Vulnerably sharing, "You know, I've been struggling so much this week ... the boys are beyond pissed at me for hiring you."

"That's normal, I'm a new person. No one likes change, especially teenage boys."

"Yeah, but I've never seen Journey this blissfully content before. It's like you're her new favorite human."

"It may—"

"No," she chimed in, shaking her head. "Don't do that. Don't devalue what you're doing in this house, Camila. I love that she's already fond of you. You're going to need a teammate."

"That bad, huh?"

"Yeah... Jagger is just, well ... he follows Jackson's lead because he's the oldest, so whatever he says, goes. And Jackson ... he's just ... a little shit right now."

I smiled, dripping of sarcasm. "I can't wait."

She laughed, rubbing Journey's back. "I'm happy she's happy."

I nodded, looking down at piercing blues that reminded me of her daddy. "Girls against boys, yeah?"

She giggled, and I swear she gave me a slight wink.

For the next few hours, Skyler showed me around the house again, except this time she really went in depth about what I was responsible for.

Cleaning.

Keeping up with laundry.

Cooking.

Housekeeper duties with nanny obligations is what she told me.

Everything and anything when it came to the kids and absolutely nothing pertaining to Dr. Pierce or his wife. It was as if they didn't exist, and I was beginning to wonder if they even did.

If it wasn't for their bedroom I wasn't allowed in, I'd think Skyler made them up. But I guess someone was floating the bills for this huge house and my salary which wasn't cheap by any means.

I spent most of the morning resisting the urge to ask a bazillion questions about where they were. Instead, I refocused my attention on the kids and making their house a home.

Besides, I was sure my questions would be answered soon enough. At least I hoped they would.

Little Miss and I went right to work on cleaning the pigsty of a home she'd been living in. We started off in the bedrooms and slowly but surely moved our way around the house.

In between feedings and naps, Journey was with me. Hanging off this brand new, never opened kangaroo pouch thing I found in her closet. She loved every second of the fast-paced day we were leading to get the house cleaned.

My goal was to have it spic and span so I could focus on the laundry tomorrow, and still have time to fix dinner for the boys, before I left for the night.

Prioritizing was a must.

Sometime in the afternoon, Skyler ran out to do some errands, letting me know she'd be back before the boys were home from school. We waved her off and continued on our mission.

"Alright, Miss Thang," I said to Journey, pulling her out of the pouch on my chest. "How about we kick up the mood around here?"

She excitingly kicked her legs. "Gah!"

"My thoughts exactly."

I set her in her glider in the living room, grabbed my phone out of the back pocket of my jeans, and plugged it into the radio.

After figuring out how to work the thing, I hit play on my cleaning playlist, and house music by Eddie Thoneick blared off the speakers in the open room between us.

Journey instantly started giggling and babbling, and once again, I swear she started shaking her booty like me. The girl was after my very own heart.

"Oh, I see you, gurl! You like to dance, huh?" I grabbed her chubby little arms, clapping her hands together to the beat of the tune. "Like this." Rocking my hips, left to right, I twirled around in a body roll for her.

She beamed.

"That's the washing machine move. Stick with me, Little Miss, and your milkshake will bring all the boys to the yard."

She fell into a fit of giggles, throwing her head back.

This baby was a genius.

"This is another one, I call it the booty pop. Ready?"

"Gah!"

It was all the affirmation I needed to continue my swaying for her. The song played on as did my dancing-slash-cleaning steps. At one point, I even grabbed the Windex and sprayed it on the windows while shaking my tatas and showing her my wax on, wax off moves.

Journey giggling and having the time of her life was reason enough to keep me dancing for her. For the life of me, I didn't want it to stop.

"Alright, now this, baby girl, this is what brings all the boys to my yard. You ready?"

"Gah!"

The beat dropped fast. Except this time, I shook my money makers in sync with my hips. Almost like I was doing the limbo, getting lower and lower to the floor beneath me.

"Now this is my closing move, Journey. This seals the deal, ya feel me?"

"Bah!"

"You ain't ready! You ready?"

"Bah! Gah! Bah!"

Right then and there, I was about to show her my Shakira moves but when I looked up, I came face to face with the boys.

Jackson...

And

Jagger.

"Oh crap," I whispered to myself, hauling ass to the radio. I instantly shut it off, quickly realizing Skyler had just walked in too. Her eyes trying to figure out what was going on.

I opened my mouth to explain, but Jackson beat me to it and brought our attention over to him.

With his phone aimed directly at me, he stated, "Thanks, Skyler, for hiring us our own private stripper."

My mouth dropped open, was he recording me?

"Jackson, that's not what I was doing. I was dancing for Journey and making her laugh."

He cunningly grinned and abruptly turned and left, Jagger followed close behind him. His head hanging low, but it was the soft chuckle and smile on Jagger's face that had me smiling and chuckling too.

For some reason, I just knew it was the first time he'd laughed or smiled in who knows how long. As embarrassed as I was, it didn't take away from the fact...

That I at least got two Pierces to laugh and smile on my first day.

Even if it was at my expense.

Camila

Now

By the time I walked through the hallway of my apartment complex later that day, it was well after nine at night.

"Oh, hell no," I murmured, noticing the door to my place was unlocked when I went to turn the key and that only meant one thing.

As soon as I opened the door and stepped inside, I stopped dead in my tracks. My head jerked back, my eyes almost fell out of their sockets. Taking in the large stacks of money laid out before me on my coffee table.

"Sean," I hissed, shifting my eyes to his large frame sitting on my couch nonchalantly, like it was no big deal there were thousands of dollars laid out in front of us.

"It ain't what ya think, baby."

"Is that right? Care to enlighten me then? 'Cuz I know your ass didn't break into my apartment to hide your blood money here."

"I ain't hidin' shit. It's for you."

"It's for me? What the hell does that mean?"

"It means, it's yours. It's for your nursin' loans. You ain't gotta work at another man's house, I'll take care of you. Alright?"

"Oh, fuck no," I seethed, slamming the door behind me. I was over to him in two long strides, stepping right up in his face. "Who the hell do you think you are, Sean?"

He stood up, stepping into mine. His giant build towered over my five-feet-four frame, but I didn't back down. If anything, I stood taller. Cocking my head in his face.

"I'm your man, that's who."

"You haven't been my man in a really long time, so quit with the bullshit. Get out of my apartment and take your drug money with you."

He grinned, licking his lips. "You know what your feisty Latina temper does to me, Camila. So how 'bout I just slip you the D to shut ya the fuck up."

I pushed him, hard. He barely wavered, pissing me off even more. "I don't want to catch anything, Sean. Why don't you hit up your groupies? Plenty of them live in this building. I mean, I'm just basing it off the times you stumbled from my bed into theirs."

"Baby, how many times do I have to tell you? You've always been my number one girl. Gettin' my dick sucked here and there don't change the fact you're my queen." He lifted his hand to touch me, and I shoved it away. "You just tryin' to make my dick hard."

"Try touching me one more time and watch what I do to your hard dick. Now. Get. Out!"

"I ain't goin' nowhere." He sat his stubborn ass back down, placing his arms out on the back of the couch.

My couch.

"Comfortable, Sean?"

"I will be once ya get on your knees."

"And do what exactly?"

"Thank me for payin' off your student loans."

"I'm not taking your money."

"Jesus Christ, Camila! Just take the fuckin' money and appreciate that you got a man who takes care of what's *his*."

There was no getting through to him when he got like this. It was the biggest problem with our relationship. Him thinking he owned me. With ownership came control, and with control came dominance...

Over me.

Sean didn't want an equal partner, he wanted a fucking groupie who tended to his every burning desire.

Hood rat wifey material.

Umm ... no thank you.

"I stopped fuckin' wit' you 'bout school, didn't I? If you want to waste your time and my money than so be it. But I want you home raisin' our babies, not some fuckin' doctor's, who lives in a white rich ass neighborhood in Oak fuckin' Island."

I gritted, clenching my jaw. "Sean, how the hell do you know the town I'm working in?"

"Camila, quit playin'. Do you want me to tell you his address too? Don't act like I don't know every last thin' 'bout you. I need to protect what's mine. Now get the fuck outta my sight and go make me a sandwich. Your man's hungry."

The audacity of this asshole never ceased to amaze me.

"You know what?"

"What, baby?"

"I think it's time for you to eat your dinner out."

"Cami—"

I abruptly turned, grabbing as many stacks of bills that would fit into my arms.

"Camila, don't you fuckin' try me!" Sean yelled, knowing exactly where I was taking his blood money.

"It's time for you to go." I opened the door and chucked the pile of cash into the hallway.

Making it rain down the stairwell.

He darted after the money. "You crazy bitch!"

"Awe ... Sean," I mocked, throwing the rest of the cash into the hallway right next to him. "But I thought I was your *queen*." I flung his gym bag at his chest and he caught it midair. "Byeeeee."

"Cam—"

I slammed the door in his face, quickly locking it behind me. Making a mental note to have the locks changed.

Again.

"This ain't over!" he roared, banging on the door.

"It is for now!" I hollered back, slamming my fist against the hard wood.

I was playing with fire, but Sean would never physically hurt me. At least not intentionally. A girl could only take so much, and I'd reached my limit. He'd be back, though. Sean was like a pesky fly I couldn't swat away or kill. No matter how hard I tried.

I waited by the door until I heard his footsteps descend the stairs, and his profanity become nothing but an echo. Making sure he was really gone before I went about my business. I hated that he thought he held so much power over me. I was just supposed to get on my knees and thank him for his hustling ways.

Who knows where that money came from, because I sure as shit know he didn't legally work for it. Sean could shove his money where the sun didn't shine. I could take care of myself.

Always had, always would.

On top of having to deal with the piece of shit that was my ex, I finished off my day at the Pierces explaining myself to Skyler. I was just dancing for the baby, making her laugh. I must have lost track of time, hence the boys walking in. She understood, saying her kids loved to dance too. Ending our conversation with pointers on how to handle Jackson.

"Be patient with him…"

"He'll come around…"

"He's just taking his frustrations out on you."

I appreciated her input, but if I wanted Jackson to respect me, I had to beat him at his own game.

Plain and simple.

If he thought an insult was going to make me run for the hills, he had another thing coming. The boy was in for a rude awakening, and I had no problem being the one who delivered it.

Bang! Bang! Bang!

The loud knocking from the other side of the door, tore me away from my thoughts.

Followed by Danté shouting, "Camila! Open up!"

"Sean out there with you?"

"Gurl, you know I don't fuck wit' Sean! Open the damn door, I got somethin' to show you."

I rolled my eyes, getting up to open it. Danté quickly strolled inside, turning to face me when I closed the door behind him.

"Camila, mamita, you know you're shakin' dat ass on YouTube?"

"What?" I scoffed, confused.

"You heard me." He showed me the screen on his phone. "See for yourself."

My mouth dropped open, witnessing with my own two eyes my dancing from this afternoon. Titled, *"Nannies Gone Wild."*

"That little shit!" I snarled, snatching the phone out of his grasp.

For the next ten minutes, I watched in complete disbelief how much Jackson recorded. The worst part was the video already had thousands of views in the matter of a few hours.

"I'm going to strangle him! Be patient, my ass!"

Danté chuckled, "Look on the bright side, at least you look good shakin' dat ass! You're like a ho turned into a housewife. I mean damn, gurl, you on point with dem moves."

"Danté…"

"I'm serious. Think 'bout all the tips you gonna get at my club now. Honey, you good for business."

"That's if Dr. Pierce doesn't fire me first."

"If you get fired, it ain't gonna be 'cuz of Dr. Pierce," he mumbled under his breath. "Just sayin'."

"Oh my God." I hit my forehead with the palm of my hand. "Mrs. Pierce is going to be the one who fires me, isn't she?"

"I mean … weren't you tellin' me last night that neither of them are around? Maybe they won't see it. But if they do…" He shrugged. "Doctor Daddy gonna be savin' this for his spank bank later. Best believe that, mamita."

"Eww!"

"Camila, why you messin' wit' me? You know I Googled his ass. That man fine. Quit playin' like you haven't noticed how fine that man is."

Of course, his nosy ass would have snooped. "Thanks for invading my privacy."

"There's no privacy among besties. We family, for life."

"Shit…" I fell back onto my couch. "What do I do now?"

He fell beside me on the sofa, tugging me to his side. "First, the video is not that bad, I'm just playin' wit' you. But for real, just to be one hundred wit' you, those boys are watchin' way worse on their phones than just you dancin' around."

"Gross."

"They're boys."

"Enough said."

"Camila, mamita, first lesson of thinkin' like a punk ass kid is that boy be tryin' to hold one over you. So, beat him at his own game."

"You mean…"

"That's exactly what I mean. Come on, honey, lets show him who he's workin' wit'."

Waking up bright and early the next morning, I made it to his bus stop with plenty of time to spare, so I could chat with my new pain in the ass.

"Jackson!" I hollered, dragging his attention from his friends.

"Ooooohhhh weeee!" they chanted and cheered, noticing immediately who I was.

Boys.

Jackson was the only one who seemed genuinely caught off guard by me standing several feet away from them. Putting enough distance between us to confront him in private. They were all proudly wearing football jerseys, thinking they were the shit.

Ah, so Jackson was a football star...

The little shit smirked as if he could read my mind while eyeing a girl around his age who was standing with her own friends, further away from him. He arrogantly winked at her before making his way over to me with the same swagger of a man.

Was he trying to make her jealous?

With me?

What the hell was that?

When he greeted me a little too loudly with, "Hey, baby, you here to dance for me and my friends?" I knew exactly what he was trying to pull.

"Why don't you show them the moves you've been perfecting with Dance Revolution on your Xbox."

His eyes widened, and his face turned a bright shade of red.

"Oh, I'm sorry. Was that a secret? Jackson if you needed dance lessons you could have just asked me. No need to film me to learn a few moves."

"Shut up," he warned under his breath.

"But, Jackson? What am I going to do with this new dance footage I have for you?" I didn't have any new footage for him, but he didn't have to know that. "I'm only trying to help you find the rhythm you're obviously lacking based on the level your game is at. Beginners 101—"

He stepped toward me. "I mean it, shut your mouth, Camila."

"Oh, so you do know my name?" I replied in a much softer tone. "I couldn't tell with how many times you called me Mary Poppins in the comments section."

"What do you want?"

"Take the video down or I'll out you to your friends with how many dancing games you really do have."

"It's not what you think."

"Hey, guys—"

"They were my mom's," he interrupted, rendering me speechless. "I'll take it down, alright? Now leave."

"Jackson, did you just say they *were* your mom's?"

"I said, *leave*. You don't know shit."

"I'm just trying to help."

"Then why don't you go shake your ass on a pole where you belong, instead of at my house where nobody wants you."

I frowned, unable to form words. Swallowing hard, I watched him walk away. Feeling at a loss.

Jackson: 1

Me: 0

I spent the rest of the day feeling like the piece of shit he wanted me to feel like. Focusing only on what he said to me.

"They were my mom's."

AIDEN
Then: Almost twelve-years-old

"Get out of here, you little shit!" Mr. Byron shouted, slamming his fists down on the dining room table near five-year-old Nathan, making Bailey jump out of her skin.

I tried not to let it get to me, needing to stay strong for her. It was the only thing I had to offer. It was always the only thing I had to give her.

No one wanted us.

No one loved us.

No one protected us.

All we had was each other.

I hugged her, bringing her closer to my body.

Harder.

Tighter.

Firmer.

Needing to have her heartbeat next time to mine. It was the only time I knew we were alive.

She struggled to breathe.

To see.

To feel me against her.

"Bailey, please … it's going to be alright."

She cried, breaking apart in my arms.

"Boy, don't make me tell you again! Get the fuck out of my sight, before I show you who's boss around here!"

"Byron! Just leave—"

"You stupid bitch! Did I tell you to move? Did I give you permission to say a damn thing?"

"Byron, please calm down," his wife, Carly, whimpered.

I knew he wouldn't grant her any mercy, he never granted anyone mercy. Not even innocent kids.

We sank back further into the closet we were hiding in together. All the way back in the darkness shielded by stale-smelling clothes and coats, where no one could find us. It had become our favorite hiding spot, pretending we were the kids in the wardrobe from the book *The Chronicles of Narnia*, we read in Mrs. Jenner's fifth grade class. Praying to be transported anywhere but here when Mr. Byron drank too much. The second he started yelling and hitting anyone in his sight.

We hated him.

The man was an asshole who was never nice to any of us. All he did was sit on his lazy ass, day in and day out, barking orders at his wife with a twelve pack of beer always close by his side.

The house was old and falling apart and smelled like dirty socks and moldy food all the time. We never understood why they kept taking in more kids if he didn't want us there to begin with.

Being in the system for the last four years was a living, breathing nightmare that held us hostage against our will. Where we could never escape, never fully wake up, never get a moment of peace.

To speak our minds.

To have a say.

To know someone was on our side.

"I won't let anyone hurt you, Bay. I promise."

"Stop it!" Carly screeched, her voice laced with terror and defeat.

"Cover your ears," I ordered her. "Like I showed you."

"Fuck you!" he roared, calling her every name in the book. The sound of dishes breaking on the tile floor followed by ear-piercing screams filled the small space.

I never covered my ears like I made Bailey. I needed to hear, to make sure what his next move would be to keep us both safe. I heard it all.

Every vicious word.

Every blow to their bodies.

Every whimper.

Every sob.

Every time they begged, pleaded, prayed to God to make him stop.

"He's hurting her, Aiden. He's really hurting her this time."

"I know. It'll be over soon. Just hold on for a few more minutes, okay? Go to your happy place."

We'd been living with the Byrons for the past year. Before them, it was another shitty family, the Smiths. Before the Smiths, it was the Hunters, and the list went on with how many shitty families we'd been placed with.

Moved without notice, each time praying we'd hit the lottery of foster homes and get a decent family who'd love us, or at least care.

It wasn't all that bad. Misty was always able to pull some strings to place Bailey and me in the same temporary homes, which was all we wanted.

In four years, we'd been placed in six different foster homes and five different schools.

The foster parents who were supposed to be taking care of us never did.

They drank.

They smoked.

They did drugs instead.

Someone should have done something, but no one ever did.

We never told Misty or any of the other kids' caseworkers what we saw, or what was actually happening in these homes they believed were safe. Pretending as if life was perfect anytime someone stopped by to check on us. Terrified if we did tell them the truth, they'd split us up.

Each time they moved us, Bailey and I shared the only black trash bag we owned. Not having any proper luggage to go house to house to house in.

Each time they moved us, not all our stuff went with us. Most of our hand-me-downs got left behind for the next kid to wear them.

Each time they moved us, we lost a little more hope, a little more of our dreams, a little more...

Everything.

No one to tell us "I love you."

No one to tell us "Happy birthday."

No one to tell us we were going to be okay.

There was no one…

But *us*.

Our prized possessions never left that trash bag, afraid we wouldn't be able to grab them in time when we were escorted out. My book, blanket and pillow, picture frame, and Bailey's heart necklace were the only items that meant anything to us anyway.

"Aiden, I'm scared," Bailey whispered, breaking my heart a little more. "I'm really scared."

Even if we broke our silence, it wouldn't change anything.

They weren't really there to see…

Even if they asked.

Even if they listened.

They wouldn't care about our story.

They hadn't seen what we'd seen.

Heard what we'd heard.

Felt what we'd felt.

No one could truly understand what it was like for us, because at the end of the day…

It wasn't their problem, it was ours, and only ours. There were thousands of kids just like us, floating around the system. Waiting for a new mom and dad to choose them. Disappointed when the kid they shared a room with was picked over them. The truth was, the older you became the more hope of being adopted faded. You were the bottom of the barrel, being older secured us that spot.

"You worthless piece of shi—"

"Bay, guess what? I got an A on my math test," I shared, distracting her from the reality of our life.

"You did?" She sniffled, gazing up at me with hope in her eyes.

"I did. You know what that means?"

"You can test out of sixth grade math now?"

"Yeah."

"Really?"

"Yes. So now I'm closer to finishing school and can take care of us quicker."

"You swear?"

"I wouldn't lie to you. Ever. I'm going to buy us the house of your dreams one day, Bay."

"The one with the white picket fence and red door?"

"That's exactly the one. Your happy place."

"You promise, promise?"

"Cross my heart."

"Can I plant a garden? One with only sunflowers?"

"I'll buy you every last sunflower I can find."

"Okay." She smiled, as I wiped away her tears.

She still looked so scared.

I desperately tried to stay strong for her, ignoring the rambling and thrashing coming from the living room through the thin ass walls.

Her arms wrapped around my neck so tightly, and for the first time in a long time, it felt like she wanted to give up. Bailey wasn't as strong as I was, and it made everything that much harder on me. I had to be her rock in order for us to survive the outcome.

"Why don't they want us, Aiden? Why doesn't anyone ever want us?"

"I want you, Bailey. I want you."

"You promi—"

BANG, BANG, BANG!

"Police! Open up!"

All the blood drained from my face, and my heart leapt up into my throat. There was no hiding it, not in a moment like this.

"Aiden, what's going on?"

The front door crashed open, rattling the whole damn house. Boxes fell from the shelves above us, and heavy footsteps were heard clear as day.

"It's not what it looks like," Mr. Byron lied through his teeth. It was exactly what it looked like.

Someone must have called the cops.

"Bailey, run!" I ordered, my voice rumbling in my head.

"What? Why—"

I threw open the closet doors just as all hell broke loose.

"Oh fuck," I heard one of the men, wearing an officer uniform, breathe out.

He stopped dead in his tracks when he saw us hiding in the closet.

"They're in here! Two of them are in here!" he shouted.

"Bailey! Go! RUN!" I charged the officer, wanting her to get a head start.

She didn't move an inch, her feet glued to the floor beneath her. Watching the scene unfold in front of her fear-stricken eyes, witnessing yet another one of our worst nightmares.

"AIDEN!" she screamed bloody murder as the officer held me back.

My stomach dropped.

My heart stopped.

Waiting for the man I knew would appear.

"Where's Misty?! I want Misty!" I demanded, trying to fight him off.

I caught sight of the black SUV through the front window. I fucking hated that car. Except, this time it wasn't just one.

There were two.

Which only meant one thing.

"NO!" I roared with every last piece of myself. "You can't take her away from me!"

I immediately thrashed my body back and forth and all around. Faster and faster. Feeling like I was about to snap.

"It's alright, we're here to help. We're here to help you!" the officer holding me captive voiced, but it didn't mean a damn thing.

I opened my eyes, taking a deep breath. My chest caving in on me. The expression on Bailey's face was one I would never forget. My eyes slowly moved toward the front door, seeing not one but two large men enter the room along with two caseworkers I'd never seen, following close behind.

It was only then that Bailey and I locked eyes, and she knew exactly what was about to go down.

"NO!" Her scream mirrored my yell from seconds ago. Her voice resonating deep in my bones.

She skidded on her knees, throwing her arms around my waist, and I swear to God, I never wanted to die more than I did in that moment.

"Grab her!" the woman demanded, and the muscle went right to work.

"No!" Bailey screamed as loud as she could when the man took ahold of her. Ripping her off me, putting up one hell of a fight.

She kicked.

She bawled.

She fought.

"Don't take me away from Aiden! Please don't take me away from him!"

Tears flooded my eyes, rolling down the sides of my face.

"Aiden, please! You promised! You promised me!"

I had no control over my emotions, hitting, punching, pushing the officer restraining me as hard as I could. My body throbbed, my heart pounded, and my head started getting dizzy the more I put up a fight.

"Son, calm down!" I heard the other woman say over the ringing in my ears.

I fought with every ounce of strength I had left inside of my now hollow shell. Still holding onto the hope I'd see Bailey again.

It was all I had left to hold onto.

She was all I had left to hold onto.

Everything else had been taken from me the same way she was being dragged out of the house.

We both shoved, slapped, and hit the men holding us prisoner, wanting to hurt them as much as they were hurting us. Not paying any mind to the throbbing pain running through my body. It was nothing compared to the knife they were stabbing into my heart.

He lifted her up into the air, tossing her over his shoulder. Bringing back flashes of me being taken away from my mother. Every emotion, every scar, every insecurity made its presence known for the millionth time in my life.

"I hate you!" she hysterically wept. "Don't touch me! I need Aiden! Please don't take him from me! He's all I have!"

"I'll find you, Bailey! I promise I won't give up until I find you again!"

I watched her lose her mind, trying to grab ahold of the front door, her fingers slipping inch by inch as they made their way out to the SUV. The scene playing out in slow motion as I screamed.

The cop let me take out my anger and despair, holding onto me, knowing if he didn't...

I'd fall apart right then and there.

There was nothing left for me to do.

Nothing I could say would change the outcome of this day.
The day…
Bailey and I were separated from each other, possibly…

Forever.

Ten

Camila

Now

"Journey, what are we going to do about your brother Jackson? How do we make him accept me?"

It'd been a month since I started working at the Pierces, and still no sight of Mr. or Mrs.

Nothing.

Not so much as a hello or a goodbye.

Most of my time was spent with Journey, quickly becoming best friends with the baby girl who had already stolen my heart. She was always the only one who was actually excited to see me walk through the door. Waiting for me with open arms and lots of sloppy kisses.

Skyler wasn't lying. From day one when we met, Journey decided I was her person. Taking it upon herself to choose me.

In the evenings, she'd start fussing like an hour or so before she knew I was leaving, making it nearly impossible for me to walk out the door. Clinging onto me for dear life, and having an absolute meltdown when Skyler reached for her to relieve me.

The truth was, I loved her as much as she loved me. Deciding to stay the night in the guest bedroom more often than not, so I wouldn't have to leave her. She'd sleep in my arms, making our unbreakable bond I'd never experienced with any other babies prior to her only get stronger. There was something about Little Miss that captured my heart and soul.

And she was aware of it too.

Which worried me, *a lot*. Her parents weren't around to nurture her. Journey's mother was supposed to be the one bonding with her, not me. She should be hearing her mother's voice, having tummy time with her, teaching her to hold her own bottle, soothing her during teething, be here for her first tooth. The first time she rolled over for me, the first time she sat up for me.

The first...

The first...

The first....

But with that said, their absence didn't stop me from experiencing these pivotal moments with her. At the end of the day, someone had to. I didn't want her to forget about her parents, I made it a point to show her the pictures on the walls at least a few times a day. Always stressing who was her mom and dad, and what they looked like so she would know when she saw them again.

I hadn't seen or heard from Sean since I threw all his money out my door, knowing he would show up when I least expected him too.

To top it all off, Jackson's words from a month ago still haunted me on a daily basis.

"They were my mom's."

The urge to snoop and find answers for myself became a ticking timebomb in my body. It was only a matter of time before my curiosity would get the best of me. I needed answers. I couldn't go on like this or shake the feeling as if I was being watched.

Now, I know that sounds absolutely absurd.

But was it?

There were things that kept happening that had me not only questioning my sanity, but my patience.

For instance, I was telling Journey the other day how much I loved chocolate and kept forgetting to bring a box of Dove ice cream for her to try. My favorite. The next morning when I came into work, there in the freezer was a box of Dove ice cream.

Or the other time I grabbed the diaper rash cream, realizing it was the one I told Journey about a few days ago. Not her usual brand. This one was gentler on her soft, baby skin.

"How does this keep happening, huh?"

Journey smiled, a huge smile. The kind that lit up the room as if she already knew the answer.

"Are you trying to tell me something? Can you talk and you've been playing me for a fool?"

"Gah!" She kicked her chubby legs.

Then there was the obvious. Jackson Pierce completely despised me. Without even trying, I'd become his number one rival, his mortal enemy. I'm talking Tom vs. Jerry, North Korea vs. South Korea, Batman vs. Joker, take no prisoners type of foes.

He was doing everything and anything in his power to get rid of me. The boy put me through the ringer each week with some sort of new war tactic to take me down, and to keep me there. He hated me in every sense of the word, and I knew he wouldn't stop until he succeeded in executing me indefinitely.

And by that, I meant me quitting.

Journey really was the only ally I had in this house other than Skyler, but she didn't know what Jackson was doing to me. If I told her, it meant the little shit won, and there wasn't a chance I was going to let that happen.

Being raised in a house full of kids running around all over the place, I learned a thing or two about retaliation. I'd been through far worse than a demon spawn trying my patience.

My brothers taught me at an early age what survival was. They'd babysit me till my parents got home, pulling stunt after stunt to see what a five-year-old girl could endure. They used to take a large cardboard box laying around and line it with a bunch of pillows. I'd get in, put on my Papa's motorcycle helmet, and hug my knees to my chest.

I remember being so nervous but wouldn't voice it, I was tough, and I wanted to prove I could withstand anything. They'd close the box up tight so all I could see was darkness besides a little ping of light coming through a small air hole.

Suddenly, the box would move along the floor beneath me and I'd hear my brothers laugh and whisper, "Hold on tight."

Next thing I knew, I was flying down a flight of stairs, bouncing side to side. Sometimes even flipping several times, landing at the bottom of the stairs in a heap of cardboard and pillows.

At least they thought to protect my head, I gave them credit for that. It was their idea of fun, convincing me at the age of five that fear was simply unacceptable. Never back down from anyone.

Ever.

Jackson's scare tactics never ceased to amaze me, though. I swear they were getting more and more inventive as the weeks went by. His creativity knew no bounds.

The first week it was the YouTube video which he did end up taking down. Only after it already had thousands of views on it.

Although, it wasn't as bad as it sounded. In the long run, it worked in my favor. When I was bartending at Danté's club, if I didn't stay at the Pierces, I was making a killing. My YouTube fans were loyal and big tippers.

However, it was the second week that genuinely took me by surprise. I wasn't expecting him to continue our World War III battle. The little shit tricked me, using his charm and my stupidity, thinking we'd reached a peace treaty.

Oh, how wrong I was…

"Little Miss, I know you want me to hold you, but I have to cook," I explained, trying to calm down an unhappy baby in her glider. "I can't hold you and cook, it's too dangerous. I'm making fajitas and the oil—"

"I'll watch the stove for you while you tend to Journey," Jackson offered, catching me off guard.

I turned to find him leaning against the fridge with his arms folded over his chest.

"You will?" I replied, looking him in the eyes.

He shrugged. "Yeah."

"Why?"

He smiled, showing me his pearly white teeth. "It's the least I could do after what I did to you … you know, with the video."

"Yeah, that was kind of a dick move."

He narrowed his eyes at me, appreciating I was talking to him like a man and not like a child. Jackson was no kid, he didn't even look like most almost-thirteen-year-olds. He was definitely big for his age.

"What can I say? I can be an asshole."

"Clearly."

He smiled again, this time his eyes beamed. "You didn't deserve it. You're only here because of Skyler, we're just a job to you."

"What?" I shook my head. "No, Jackson, that's not true at all. You're not just a job to me. I'm here because I want to be. I want to help you. Your family. It's obvious there's more going on here than anyone is letting on. I mean for starters, where are your pare—"

He abruptly pushed off the fridge, ending our conversation by saying, "Journey needs you now. I'll watch the food."

Journey let out the loudest wail, agreeing with him.

"Alright, I'm going to go change her diaper. Just yell if you—"

"I can handle food, Camila."

"Right, okay. I'll be back."

"Take your time."

That should have been my first indication, the sweet talking, the smiling, the understanding … he was trying too hard. And I fell for his act.

Hook, line, and sinker.

The little terrorist dumped every hot sauce imaginable into the food I was cooking. I spent over three days trying to get my taste buds back. Did I fail to mention, I was also pissing hot sauce when I went to the bathroom? Though nothing outdid the hours I spent trying to get the fire sensation out of my mouth and nose.

After, I threw up, out of said *mouth* and *nose.*

I was a hot mess, literally.

As retribution, I fed it to him the next day. Sneaking it into his sandwich for lunch at school. Carelessly forgetting to pack him a drink with it.

Ever since then he's packed his own lunch.

Jackson: 2

Me: 2

Even battlefield.

By the third week, there was a mutual understanding that our war had only just begun. Jackson decided to take it upon himself to play professor and scribbled and messed up all my anatomy notes for my nursing class. I could have strangled him, they were the only notes I had to study from.

Needless to say, I failed the impromptu quiz the next day.

While I sulked over the fact that it was the first test I'd ever bombed, I savored in the thought of Jackson's face when he opened his gym bag for football practice. Wrapped in his jersey was an entire box of tampons covered in Kool-Aid, but he didn't know that.

The expression on his face as soon as he rushed through the door later that day, darting straight to his precious room, was enough to have Journey and I laughing our cute little booties off for hours on end.

"Got 'em, Journey!" I celebrated, blowing raspberries on her belly.

Jackson: 3

Me: 3

Once again, we were even.

He should have known better than to mess with someone twice his age. I was older, wiser, and knew how to fight dirty if need be.

Call me the Yoda of comebacks. It was the only way I survived being raised in a home filled with boys, who were all jokesters and loved to pick on girls for shits and giggles.

We were now into the fourth week, and I'd been waiting for another one of his bombs to drop every single day. It was Friday and still nothing.

Had he given up?

Did he surrender?

Or was I going to go home and step in a pile of shit he may have planted in my apartment?

A little farfetched but who knew with this kid.

I may have been the head of the Jedi, but he had Luke Skywalker's power to put up one hell of a fight with no end in sight.

And we had no Darth Vader playing mediator.

Jagger kept his head down with a smile and a laugh, and Journey...

Well, she was too little to understand anything other than shaking her booty when she heard music blaring.

The girl loved to dance.

We had that in common.

"But, Aunt Skyler," a girl's voice hummed through the halls from the kitchen, while I changed Journey's diaper in her nursery.

"Who's that, Little Miss?"

She baby babbled, answering my question.

"Oh really?"

"Bah!"

"Alright, alright, let's go see who's here." I picked her up and set her on my hip.

"Harley, we're just stopping in for a few minutes, I have to check on Camila before I come back for the night to relieve her," Skyler replied as we made our way down the hall to the kitchen. "Then we can go."

"But I hate Jackson! I already have to see him at school in most of my classes. I don't want to see him after school too."

"I know, sweetie, but you both need to suck it up and get over it."

"It's not me! It's him. He's evil."

Couldn't disagree with you there...

"He's just going through a lot, be patient with him."

"Be patient? Aunt Skyler, he's been evil since before his mom—"

"Camila, there you are," Skyler announced, looking over at us walking into the room.

Since before his mom what?

"Camila, this is my niece Harley. Harley, this is Camila, Jackson's—"

"Own private stripper," he interrupted with a cocky grin on his face, leaning against the wall.

"Jackson Pierce! Enough of that," Skyler scolded, but I didn't pay him any mind.

It'd only bait him.

He wasn't trying to hurt my feelings, it was Harley's he was after this time. She was the same girl from the bus stop.

"Jealous?" Jackson added, arching an eyebrow at her.

What was up with these two?

"You wish," she sassed, folding her arms over her chest.

"Oh my God, give it a rest. Why can't you guys learn to get along for the sake of our families?" Skyler questioned, coming in between them. "It would mean so much to your Uncle Noah and your father, Jackson."

"You mean my father who's never around?"

"He's around, Jackson."

"For who? Cuz it sure as shit ain't for us."

"Jackson! Watch your mouth. Your baby sister's first word is going to be a cussword with how much profanity comes out of your mouth."

"It's not any worse than what comes out of Noah's mouth."

"My husband doesn't speak like that when Journey is around."

"Bullshit, he did with us."

Harley scoffed out a giggle, smirking in that smitten kind of way. *Oh, she likes him.*

It wasn't until Skyler left the room, giving up on reprimanding Jackson, that I realized he liked her too. I listened to them from the living room, pretending to mind my own business.

"Hey, Harley, you have something in your hair," he told her.

"I do?"

"Mmm hmm."

"Where?"

"Right here."

Seconds later an ear-piercing shriek vibrated through the walls, so loud that it could be heard by the neighbors.

"Jackson Pierce! You put gum in my hair!"

I could tell by his amused tone, he was lying when he replied, "No, that's what was in your hair."

"You're such a liar!"

"Relax, it's just gum."

"I'm going to have to cut my hair now!"

"Maybe it will make your face look better."

She gasped. "There is nothing wrong with my face!"

"Yeah, if you're into ugly girls."

"I am not ugly!"

"Says who, your parents? They're supposed to say stuff like that."

She gasped again before screaming, "I hate you!"

"Yeah, well it's mutual. Here, I'll help you cut your hair."

"Get away from me!"

I was about to intervene, but Skyler beat me to it. I wish I could say I felt bad for her, but the only thing I was grateful for...

Well at least it wasn't me today.

Harley: 0

CHOOSING US

Jackson: 1

Eleven

Camila

Now

Later that day, I headed straight home from the Pierces.

Exhausted from the week and ready to change into jammies, watch TV, and chill. I was in the mood for some chick-flick drama. You know the kind that made you re-evaluate life and think love at first sight wasn't just a fairytale they sold to the masses.

I hadn't been in a relationship since Sean, and I wouldn't exactly call that a healthy one. We'd always had problems, standing on two opposite ends of the spectrum of life.

Don't get me wrong, I loved him, but I guess you could say I was never head over heels *in* love with him. He was the only man I'd ever been with, romantically and sexually. Though he was never there for me emotionally or mentally. He didn't know how to be those things, nor did he care to try.

He was a man in many aspects of life, except when it came to what I needed and wanted. He was a child. But I'd be lying if I said I didn't miss him. Because I did.

I was lonely.

I missed the companionship, a man on top of me, skin on skin contact. Sex was never our problem, most days you couldn't drag us out of the bedroom. However, that was never enough. *I* was never enough.

Our relationship was never enough for him.

He ran around on me more times than I care to remember. Several times I caught him mid-act.

What does that say about me?

I gave him all I had, and it was never good enough.

"Baby, you're my queen. I love you. You know that."

"You love me so much you decided to fuck the girl next door?"

"I'm a man, baby. I got needs."

I don't know what made me think about Sean, maybe it was the fact that all I saw all day long were pictures of the Pierces, living their happily ever after through images on the walls and when I pointed them out to Journey.

Their walls were filled with memories of happiness and better times. The way Dr. Pierce looked at his wife in those photos were scenes right out of romantic movies. A picture was worth a thousand words, and theirs spoke volumes.

I wanted a love like that.

One made out of trust, devotion, and respect.

They consumed my mind, and the more I thought about them, the heavier the desire to know where they were became. It was this elephant sitting in the room, this weight hanging on my shoulders, this burden I kept carrying on my back.

Where were they?

Did they know about me?

About their kids? And how much they needed them?

But most importantly, were they coming back?

How could a house filled with so much love, feel so damn empty?

Almost as if one of them were gone.

And the other was just...

Lost.

"Alright, Camila, you need to think about something else. You're there to watch their kids, not obsess over—" I stopped walking, taking in the scene in front of me, as I opened the door to my apartment.

There was Sean, in all his glory.

And by that, I mean he was butt-ass naked. Laying in my bed, waiting for what?

Me?

"Sean," I coaxed, on the verge of losing my shit.

"Hey, baby. Been waiting for you to get home, so you can bounce that ass on my cock."

¿Que es esto?

What is this?

"Have you lost your damn mind?" I slammed the door behind me. "Now, I'm going to have to burn my brand new sheets!"

"Quit fuckin' wit' me, Camila." He sat up, reaching for me. "Come over here and show your man how much you missed him."

"Ugh! Can you please for the love of God cover your junk! I can't yell at you properly when your dick is staring at me!"

"Ain't nothin' you haven't seen before."

"It's something I never wanted to see again. I'm serious, put some shorts on!" I threw his boxers at him, facing toward the kitchen.

"Why am I gonna throw on my drawers when your ass is supposed to be ridin' my cock?"

My eyes snapped to his. "My what? Sean, my ass is not going anywhere near your tainted dick. What could make you possibly think that?"

"Your text."

"My text? What text? I never texted you. I don't even like you, why would I text yo—" I stopped myself. "Oh, God … I'm going to strangle him!"

"The only thing you gonna to be stranglin' is my coc—"

"I didn't text you, Sean! Now get dressed!" I chucked his jeans at his head, nailing him in the face. "Get out!" Followed by his shirt and white wife beater. "Get out. Now!" I was like a woman gone mad, circling around the room grabbing all his shit. One by one throwing everything at his naked body.

A boot here and another there, nicking his dick.

"Son of a bitch!" He doubled over in pain.

"Oops … sorry not sorry."

"If you didn't text me, than who did?"

"My other pain in the ass."

"Are you seein' someo—"

"Sean," I bit. "You have one minute to leave, before I show you what I really want to do with that dirty dick of yours."

"The fuck? Woman, get your ass over here so I can make you scream my name."

"You know what? On second thought." I grabbed the lotion from my nightstand and threw it next to him on the bed. "There. You can actually go fuck yourself."

"Camila!" he roared, as I once again slammed the door behind me. Leaving him in my apartment. Knowing there was no getting through to him. He always thought with his dick and this wouldn't be any different.

I spent the night at Danté's, who spent most of the night laughing his ass off at my expense. Thinking the shit Jackson was putting me through was hilarious.

But Sean was my last straw.

Everyone had a limit, and I officially reached mine.

The next morning, Skyler handed me Journey and was on her way out. As soon as I got Little Miss down for her first nap, I went into Satan's bedroom, not bothering to knock.

"What the hell?" he gritted, jumping off his bed in his gym shorts. "You can't just barge in my room without knocking."

"You cannot invade my privacy like that, Jackson!"

"Why not?" he countered with a snide expression. "You do ours."

"I haven't done anything to deserve this level of disrespect from you!"

"You sound really bitchy, Camila. Guess 'Don't Answer' on your phone didn't lay the D down right?"

My mouth dropped open. "You cannot talk to me like that!"

"Alright, then leave."

"You'd love that, wouldn't you? For me to just quit."

"Yeah, I would," he replied with no hesitation what so ever. Walking over to his dresser to grab a t-shirt.

"And then what, Jackson? You're just going to treat the next nanny the same way? Until what? Your mom comes back? Is that why you can't stand me? Why you want me to quit so badly? Because you think it's going to make your mom come home?"

He stepped up to me, getting right in my face. "Shut your mouth, Mary Poppins. You have no idea what you're talking about."

"You're right, I don't. All I know is, if I had a kid like you, I'd leave too." I regretted the words that came out of my mouth as soon as they left my lips.

But it was the way Jackson's eyes glazed over with so much hurt, that shook me to my core. Now I had crossed the line.

"I didn't mean tha—"

"Get out!"

"Jackson, come on… you know I didn't mean that."

"I don't know shit."

"Exactly! Because you haven't taken the time to actually get to know me. You spend all your time and energy hating someone you won't even give a chance. I'm just trying to help you."

"I don't need your help!"

"Then what, Jackson? You're just going to spend the rest of your life, not needing anyone? Is that the way you want to live?"

"I said get out!" he snarled through a clenched jaw. His fists pumping at his sides.

"Or what? Huh? What are you gonna do? I'm not scared of you. If anything, I feel bad for you. You push everyone away. Every single person. Including your own family. One day you're going to need them, and I hope it's not too late. Because regardless of the bullshit you keep putting me through, I'm not going anywhere. I love your baby sister, and if you gave me half the chance, I could be here for you too."

He shook his head in disgust and disdain. "I don't need your pity. So why don't you go sell your spiel to someone who gives a shit about you? Because we both know, I sure as hell don't."

I jerked back, not hiding how much that hurt me. "I'm sorry your parents aren't around, okay? But it's not my fault. I didn't make them go away, Jackson. I was hired because they're not here. You need to realize that and stop blaming me for things that are out of my control."

I took a deep breath, stepping back toward the door. Not allowing the anger rolling off my body to take over, even though I wanted nothing more than to shake the shit out of him. Make him see reason.

I wasn't the bad guy.

He was just treating me like I was.

"Don't ever touch my phone again. Do you understand me?"

He eyed me up and down, cocking his head to the side. Taking in what I just said with as much curiosity as I had about his parents.

"There's a reason his name is under 'Don't answer' in my phone. You could have…" I sighed, being at my wits end.

"Who is he?"

"Someone I want nothing to do with."

"Huh, well then maybe now you'll understand. Seeing as I want nothing to do with you. Now get out."

"Alright." I nodded. "I'll get out of your room, but I'm not getting out of your life. I'm here to stay."

"Yeah, for Journey."

"And for *you*." With that, I turned around and left him there, praying something I said may have gotten through to him.

Knowing I probably wasn't that lucky.

I tried to calm down as best as I could before going back into the living room, but it was the look on Jagger's face in the hallway that pulled my attention to him instead.

"He wasn't always like this, Camila."

I swear it was the first words this kid had ever spoken to me. And there I was, glued to the floor, waiting for him to say something else. Like he was the Dalai Lama who held all the answers. Jagger kept to himself, didn't say much. Half the time, I forgot he existed, he was that quiet.

"He's mad at my dad. It's not you. Journey really loves you. You make her happy. My mom didn't have the chance to do that, and Journey is one of the reasons my dad isn't around."

I grimaced, understanding what he had just openly shared. I mean, I assumed Dr. Pierce had never held his baby girl, and now I knew he really hadn't.

But why?

"It doesn't matter what you say or do, my mom isn't coming home. That much I can tell you."

"Is she—"

"I'm sorry Jackson is treating you like this, but Journey isn't the only one who wants you here."

"She isn't?"

"No. I want you here too."

"You do?"

"Yeah."

"Why?"

"Because I think you could fix things."

"With Jackson?"

"Yeah. And maybe my dad."

"Jagger, what do you—"

He cut me off by turning around and leaving me there. Walking back into his room.

If that wasn't the most cryptic conversation I'd ever had, then I didn't know what was. I spent the entire day in a fog, contemplating my next move. Still feeling as though I was being watched. It didn't help that the books I'd been telling Journey about were sitting on her book shelf. Staring me right in the face when I went to wake her up. I must not have noticed them before, too pissed at Jackson.

"It doesn't matter what you say or do, my mom isn't coming home. That much I can tell you."

By the end of the day, there was only one thing that I was certain of. I was going to get answers. Even if I had to look for them...

Myself.

AIDEN
Then: Almost fourteen-years-old

In a two-year span, since the first time Bailey and I were split up, I hadn't seen her in a few weeks. Not from lack of trying, though. Social services fucking moved me again. This time into a shittier house with a foster family that wanted me less than the previous lowlifes I'd been living with before them. At least my old family had lived closer to Bailey's current foster placement. The last five she'd been moved from were all over the place. It was hard to keep up, but I kept my promise to her.

I found her.

Every. Single. Time.

No matter where she was, I made it a priority to see her, be with her when I could.

Our caseworkers began to change as quickly as our foster homes. Proving age was just another drawback to this fucked up system we lived in.

I'm sure there may have been some good foster homes out there, but we sure as shit never saw them. Those homes wanted newborns, toddlers, and kids who hadn't experienced too much trauma brought on by their own parents or the foster homes they were being placed in.

Misty was no longer around, becoming just another person who left my life without a moment's notice. No goodbye, nothing. I never saw her again, neither did Bailey.

All we had was each other.

When my head wasn't buried in books, studying for all my advanced honor classes in school, I spent my free time trying to figure out how to get to Bailey on my bike.

That day came when I found an old map of the area in Mr. Dale's so-called office space. I spent every waking moment mapping out the best route. Determined to get to her no matter what stood in my way.

It was Christmas Eve, I had to see my girl.

With my worldly possessions and Bailey's Christmas present in an old backpack, I pedaled to her. I didn't trust anyone in the homes I was placed in, not to steal the couple of items I did own. They went everywhere with me. It was hard enough trying to stay invisible to the adults and other foster kids who wanted nothing more than to tear me apart.

Day in and day out.

It didn't matter that it took over an hour of hardcore pedaling to see her beautiful face again. I'd scour the world for Bailey if that was what it took.

She was mine.

She was all I had.

My best friend, my family, my inside and out.

We tried making it a point to talk on the phone every night at exactly eight o'clock, no matter what. Both of us needing to check in with one another, mostly for our own peace of mind. It made things easier, knowing someone else in the universe loved and cared for you.

When you're told on a daily basis you're worthless, you'll amount to nothing, and no one gives a flying fuck about you.

It's hard to tell yourself not to believe it.

To fight for a better tomorrow, a brighter future, *a home.*

Bailey would be my home, and I'd be hers. I'd make it happen, I had to.

For the both of us.

"Aiden, where are we going?" Bailey whined, tugging on my hand to slow down. Trying to get me to answer for what felt like the hundredth time in a matter of minutes. It became evident early on that my girl had no patience, and I swear she only got worse as the years went on.

I checked on her surprise I'd been working on in the woods, before I got relocated again, making sure it was still good to go. Trying to ignore the uneasy feeling in the pit of my stomach, until I actually got to see her standing in front of me, unharmed.

Since the first time we got separated and I could no longer make sure she was alright by seeing her and making sure she was safe, Bailey picked up the habit of making everything seem fine when it wasn't. So she wouldn't worry me, never realizing her well-being always worried me.

Our lives were far from fine, and no amount of bullshit coming from her mouth would ever make me think otherwise.

But my girl had a heart of gold, and because of that she'd hide things from me all the time. Like the time one of her foster guardians slapped her across the face for accidentally throwing his cigarettes out. When he should have been grateful she was cleaning up the piss-poor excuse of a roof he claimed he was providing over her head.

She lied, telling me she fell off the bed she shared with two other girls, knowing I'd lose my shit if I knew the truth. Except, Bailey couldn't lie worth shit. I saw right through it, I always did. Although that didn't stop her half-ass attempts of trying to keep stuff from me.

Case in point, I had to see her with my own two eyes to believe her.

Needing to make sure she was really fine, and she wasn't just trying to blow smoke up my ass.

"Bay, don't worry about it. How many times do I have to tell you? When you're with me, you never have to worry about anything. I got you, Bay." I turned and winked at her, squeezing her hand in reassurance. "I always got you. Me and you against the world, remember?"

She beamed with a familiar gleam in her eyes that got me through the hard nights. Thinking about Bailey's smile, her laugh, the way she lit up just for me ... that shit got me through a lot of nights, a lot of days, a lot of *everything.*

I smiled at her one last time and continued walking through the dark woods as she followed close behind, carefully stepping in my tracks.

Mother Nature chose Christmas Eve to unleash her wintery fury in North Carolina, practically shutting down the whole state. The ground was covered in frost, blanketed by a dusting of snow while huge, soft flakes fell from the night's sky. The frozen fluff crunched under our boots with each step we treaded deeper into the forest. I held her hand tighter so she wouldn't slip on the fallen branches coated with a thin layer of ice.

"Aiden, I have to tell you something," she uttered out of nowhere.

My heart dropped, and I stopped dead in my tracks, causing her body to collide with mine. Fearing the worst.

She instantly called me out on it, "No! It's not anything like that." Turning me to face her, fully aware of where my mind went to first.

One of my biggest fears was that Bailey would get molested or raped by a foster guardian or a foster sibling. Which happened to kids…

All. The. Time.

"Bay, don't start sentences like that," I stated, my tone still shaken up.

"I know, I know. I'm sorry, I wasn't thinking. And it's Christmas and you're here, and I just… I don't… I mean…"

I grabbed her chin, rubbing my thumb against her cheek through the worn, tattered hole in my glove. "What's up, Bay? You can tell me anything."

"I know. It's just…" Her eyes brimmed with fresh tears. "I don't have a gift for you, Aiden. I'm sorry. I was going to buy you a new hoodie from the thrift store down on Main since you gave me the only one you own when it started getting cold out. But I couldn't save enough money from walking Nina's dog from next door."

My eyes shifted to the hoodie she was talking about. It looked more like a dress on Bailey, but it kept her warm which was all that mattered. She had less clothes than I did, everything she owned was very worn hand-me-downs and not in good shape by any means.

Besides, I loved seeing her in my clothes.

It always did something to me.

109

"Bay, how many times do I have to tell you to stop walking that damn dog? It walks *you*. I don't need a gift from you. I'll have some extra money next time to hold you over until I see you again."

"Aiden, you can't keep giving me money. I need to make my own. You don't earn that much as it is with whatever you end up doing. It's not fair—"

The expression on my face was enough to render her speechless. "I'm just saying…" she muttered loud enough for me to hear.

"I know what you're saying, and I'm sorry, Bay, but I don't give a fuck. I'm going to give you money, and you're going to take it. Just because you're wearing layers of clothing, doesn't mean I can't tell you've lost more weight. Are those motherfuckers even feeding you?"

"There's ten of us in the house now, and—"

"Ten?! They took in more kids? Of course, they did, greedy fucks," I breathed out, trying to control my temper. Not letting the reality of our lives ruin the moment I wanted to have with her.

The one I'd been dreaming of since the first time she shared her plate of food with me under the green slide.

"Aiden, they're younger and need more food than I do."

"You know what I need, Bay? I need you alive."

"You're exaggerating."

"And you're downplaying the situation like you always do with everything."

She took a deep breath and narrowed her eyes at me. "Fine. I'll eat more, will that make you stop giving me money?"

"No, but nice try."

"Oh. My. God! You're impossible! Do you even hear yourself? We're supposed to take care of each other, remember? But all you do is take care of me. How's that fair to you?"

"Since when is anything fair to us? I take care of you because I can, because I want to, because one day, we won't live in this bullshit, and you'll always know I took care of you because I lo—" I stopped myself. This wasn't how I envisioned the night going down. Not by a longshot. I rubbed the back of my neck, my muscles tensed immediately. "Bailey, you know that shit doesn't matter to me. It's money. *You*, matter to me."

Her deep stare was so penetrating, so intense, that I couldn't break it. I couldn't move my eyes from hers even if I wanted to, and I didn't want to. I never did. The times with Bailey, whether good or bad, were the only ones I had to look back on when I needed a sense of hope.

A sense of belonging.

When I needed love.

When I just needed…

Her.

"Come on." I nodded toward the faint glow of lights in the distance. Smiling back at her, breaking the sudden tension between us. "We're almost there."

"This isn't over."

"*Yes*, it is."

Before she could reply, I started walking the uneven ground again, tugging her behind me. I spent all my money, from working jobs that paid me under the table, on this surprise and didn't think twice about it. I wanted her to have this special moment, to see it, to feel it, for her to experience Christmas for once in her life.

It didn't take long until we approached a small clearing where the snow continued to raise beneath our feet. The look on her face the second she saw I had turned part of the woods into a winter wonderland was the only gift I needed this Christmas.

"Aiden, I can't believe you did this," she whispered, completely caught off guard. Her eyes shifted from all the colorful lights strung around the trees, to the makeshift Christmas tree I found thrown away on a curb. Decorated with soda cans and string lights. To the plastic snowman I found thrown away on another curb.

I watched her walk around the open space, grazing her bare fingers along the lights with a beaming smile on her face. Twirling around as the snow fell upon her. Bailey captivated me all the time, consuming me with her beauty, her quirks, her loving personality that shined through since we were young.

Making her presence known whether she realized it or not. Part of me knew she was conscious of the effect she had on me. It didn't matter what she was doing, my eyes followed her everywhere, constantly waiting for her to do something else that would make me fall in love with her just a little bit more.

There was no one else in this world like Bailey, and I knew that the second I laid eyes on her almost seven years ago.

Sometimes I would watch her from across the room and just the vision of her left me breathless. She was turning into a beautiful young woman. There was nothing left to resemble the scared little girl, who hid with me in the closets of the shithole homes we were placed in.

"Aiden, don't let your mind go there," she stated, bringing my thoughts back to the present. Placing her cold hand on my warm cheek. You see, she had the ability to see right through me too.

"Just thinking about your pretty face."

She rolled her eyes. "Mmm hmm." Knowing I was lying. "For someone who always wants me to be honest, you should follow your own advice."

"You want honesty, Bay? That's what you're looking for?"

"Always."

"Well then, look up."

She did. Realizing there was a wrapped gift dangling from the tree branch we were standing under.

"Oh, come on. This was enough. You didn't have to get me something too."

"That's *my* gift."

She cocked her head to the side. "You got yourself a present for me to open?"

I grinned. "Open the gift, Bailey."

She eyed me skeptically then did just that. Jerking back when she realized what it was. "Aiden, why did you—"

Before the next word left her mouth, I gripped onto the back of her neck and pulled her to me.

They say the smallest decisions can change your life forever.

I would eternally remember this moment for the rest of my days. This was the instant that changed everything between us. Exactly the way I wanted it to.

Standing right then and there, under the mistletoe I wrapped for her.

I rasped, "To kiss you," against her lips. "I don't see myself when I'm with you because all I ever see… is *you*, Bay."

Not knowing what the fuck I was doing, I kissed her with everything I had inside of me. Making her knees buckle and my heart pound. I sought out her tongue, and she moaned in my mouth as both of my hands found the sides of her face and her hands found my hair, pulling at it almost instantly.

The taste of her.

The warmth, the need, the longing to make her mine.

The sensation of her pouty lips while framing her face I adored so goddamn much. My hands found their way down her body, and I wanted nothing more than to keep going, but not here.

Not like this.

This kiss would have to be enough to hold me over until the time was right to prove she was made just for me and only me.

Our lips devoured each other, both of us making a memory to take with us, not knowing when another chance would come along again where we could feel whole in one another's love. I wish I could describe the intensity I found myself going through with her in my arms. Only I couldn't even do it justice. I couldn't even put it into words what was in my heart.

What had always been there.

What would always be there.

It overpowered me.

She overpowered me.

I let it take control, and a huge part of me wanted to throw caution to the wind and just go with it.

I didn't.

Because she deserved better.

She deserved it all.

And I would be the one to give it to her.

No one else, but *me*.

Enjoying the sensation of her lips against mine one last time, I pulled away and she instantly whimpered at the loss.

"Bailey," I huskily groaned inches away from her mouth. Placing my forehead on hers with my hands still holding onto the sides of her face.

She immediately opened her dark, dilated eyes. Looking so fucking beautiful, so fucking innocent, so everything I ever needed and wanted.

"Aiden," she panted back, luring me in again.

I softly pecked her lips, rubbing mine back and forth on hers. Gazing deep into her eyes, murmuring, "I love you. I love you so much it hurts," saying it for the first time when I'd been wanting to express it all along. "You're *mine*, Bailey, and don't you ever forget that."

Except, I was wrong...

Her Christmas gift to me wasn't her reaction to my surprise or this kiss, her present to me was the second...

The moment...

The instant...

She revealed,

"I love you too."

Making this the day, we became a couple.

Thirteen

Camila
Now

Sixty days.

Eight-and-a-half weeks.

Two whole months since I started working at the Pierce residence, and despite everything Jackson was still putting me through, nothing compared to the stunt he pulled on me today.

I grabbed my phone from my purse and dialed the first person who came to mind.

"Hola, chica, que paso, mamita?"

"Danté! Oh my God, I don't know what to do! I have no idea how to get this smell out of the house!"

"Gurl, calm down. What's goin' on? You're talkin' in circles."

"I'm so screwed! How am I going to explain this? There's no way she'd believe me over him. Not about this!"

"Camila, where are you?"

"The Pierces," I muttered, feeling at a loss.

"Text me the address. I'm on my way."

"Thank you."

"Always, mamita. I got you, gurl."

I hung up and texted him the address immediately and waited on pins and needles for the next two hours for him to arrive. Killing time, keeping Journey busy outside in the backyard.

Meanwhile, trying to create a plan of action and figure out what the hell I was going to do next.

Jackson really screwed me this time.

As soon as my phone pinged with a new text message from Danté saying he was at the front door, I rushed inside with Journey in my arms.

With an amused expression on his face, he jerked back when he saw us standing there.

Imploring, "Why does that baby look like she belongs to Michael Jackson hangin' out of a window, and not a rich ass white doctor who lives in the suburbs?" he questioned, taking in the surgical mask I put on her that I found in the kitchen drawer.

I didn't hesitate in replying, "Because the house reeks of weed!"

"Gurl, since when you start tokin'?"

"Not funny!" I opened the door wider, nodding at him. "Come on, come inside."

As soon as he stepped over the threshold, he breathed out, "Dayum…" Looking all over the foyer and into the rest of the house. The amazed expression on his face mirrored the one I had the first time I walked into this house as well. "Daddy Pierce got a lot of money," he sang out loud, rocking his head side to side.

"Danté…" I coaxed, not having the patience to deal with him too. "I'm being serious. Can't you smell that?"

"Gurl," he countered with nothing but attitude in that Danté sort of way. "Ain't no one here right now, but you, me, and baby Paris."

"Her name is Journey."

"Gah!" she added for good measure.

"Damn, gurl. I drove all this way to help you, the least you could do is let me live my best life for a few minutes." He grabbed a picture of Dr. Pierce off the entry table, bringing it up to his face. "What do you think? We look good together?"

"Danté!"

"You know what they say … once you go black, you never go back. I could be his by Tuesday."

"Oh my God." I rubbed my face. "Why did I call you?" My eyes shifted toward him rushing away. "Where are you going?"

"To see how my future sugar daddy lives! Gurl, I got this! Now keep up!"

In a matter of a few seconds, I was chasing him around the house with Journey in my arms and it made it hard to keep up. He scurried around every room at warp speed, trying to take in as much as he could.

Singing, "I'm so fancy! Yes so, so fancy! In my new Barbie house! With my new Doctor Daddy!"

"Danté, no! I'm not allowed to go in—" Before I could finish what I was about to say, he opened the double doors to the master bedroom. Almost knocking me on my ass.

I watched the entire thing unfold through one of those out of body experiences. Where you know you shouldn't be doing something, but your feet move on their own accord. Slowly, I strode into the room that possibly held all the pieces to the puzzle I was still dying to figure out.

More so now than ever before.

The logical side of my brain screamed at me to get the hell out of there. To not cross the very thin line I was currently treading on.

However, the other side of my mind that controlled my curiosity said go screw yourself, we're going in there.

So, I did.

I gradually pushed the heavy wooden door open the rest of the way, cautiously stepping inside. Careful not to make any noises, any sudden movements, any disturbance that could cause ... I don't know what.

The room was dead silent, not even the sound of a clock ticking to break the stillness in the air.

Nothing.

Even Danté stopped singing, overwhelmed with the unexpected turn of events like I was.

I paid him no mind as he went around the room doing a three-hundred-and-sixty-degree twirl with his mouth wide open. I was on a completely different mission with a one-track mind to find out where Dr. and Mrs. Pierce were.

Who they were.

And if they'd be coming back to the family who still needed them.

In that moment, I thought about a million and one things, picturing a life through their eyes. Sensing their presence in every inch and corner of the extravagant space only added to the ramblings in my mind.

If I thought the house was exquisite before, nothing compared to the luxury this suite held.

It was breathtaking.

Picture-perfect.

A room where dreams were made of.

From the huge king-sized mattress that was in between a gray wooden, massive four-poster bed, centered on the far wall. To the colossal posts with intricate carved designs each appeared to have that I ran my fingers over. To the four vast beams towering up toward the vaulted ceiling, connecting above into a square. Draped with white, sheer curtains that fell to the floor near the head of the bed.

The sheets appeared as if they hadn't been slept on in months. Not to mention the room was spotless. Nothing was out of place, not a piece of clothing, or a hairbrush. Not even one of the kids' toys.

My fingers skimmed the bedding, continuing my descent. I put one foot in front of the other, walking over to the vanity in the adjacent corner. Captivated by the elegant perfume bottles in a perfect line, I brought the one that read *Sunflower* up to my nose, breathing in the flowery scent until Journey broke the silence.

"Gah! Gah, gah, gah!"

"Is that right, Little Miss? You smell your momma?"

She kicked her chubby little legs in excitement answering my question.

"Where is she?" I whispered to myself, placing the bottle back down.

I couldn't help but wander toward her walk-in closet. Which was just as immaculate as everything else. All her clothes were lined up perfectly in order, all color coordinated by style and design.

Hundreds of dresses...

Multiple racks of skirts, shirts, and shoes...

The tips of my fingers ran along the soft fabrics, wanting to see what they felt like. The expensive pieces were as inviting as anything else in the room.

I don't know what got into me, but I had to see his closet next. Except, when I slid open the door, I thought I'd find the same setup as hers.

I didn't.

His closet had very little clothing. It was empty compared to hers. I tried to ignore the masculine scent that still lingered on his casual garments hanging on suede hangers.

A few t-shirts...

Some jeans...

A pair of sneakers here and there.

All his professional attire was missing.

No collared shirts.

No suit jackets.

No dress pants.

Nothing was left of the man everyone called Dr. Pierce, as if she stayed in this sanctuary and he was...

Gone.

"When was the last time someone was in here?" Danté questioned, asking the same thing that was running wild in my mind.

"What?"

"You feel that too, right?"

"Feel what?"

"The void. The loneliness. Camila, honey, ain't no one been in this room in a long time. This ain't a bedroom, it's a mausoleum."

My eyes shifted every which way, wanting to argue, to put up a fight, to yell at him and rationalize he didn't know what he was talking about. But I couldn't get my mouth to say one word. Because in my heart, in my soul, in the core of my body, I knew he was right.

"Oh, God," I gasped, my heart breaking with their baby girl firmly placed in my arms. I panted, "We have to get out of here. We can't be in here."

"Camila—"

"Danté, now!" I yelled, causing Journey to jolt.

There was this eerie aura surrounding me. Making it hard to breathe. Hard to focus on more than one thing other than the sensation of being watched.

I felt like a fool. How hadn't I seen this coming?

The kids...

No one talking about her...

"Hold her. Please hold her."

He grabbed the baby out of my arms, and she willingly went. Reading my emotions like a book.

I retraced my steps, trying to see if I moved something out of place, or if Danté did. This felt wrong, it felt so unbelievably wrong to be in here.

Their safe haven.

Their privacy.

Their love.

It all hit me like a ton of bricks as my reflection caught the floor length mirror across from the bed. Dr. Pierce didn't come *home* for one reason and one reason only.

He didn't have *one* anymore.

His wife took it all with her.

Leaving him and their kids behind...

And all alone.

Camila

Now

"Mamita, you need to relax," Danté stressed, hovering over me while I sat on the couch in the living room. Breathing in and out.

"Danté, the house still reeks of weed. I just realized my employer may be dea... I can't even bring myself to say it."

"You gotta worry about one thing at a time. You ain't here for them, you're here for these kids."

"I know." I nodded, reaching for Little Miss who seemed to be having a great time with whatever Danté and her were up to.

"While you were havin' your pity party for one, Paris and I found the solution to your Maryjane debauchery." He showed me the Lysol All-Purpose Cleaner in one hand with a towel drenched in the liquid in his other. "Run this in the dryer, twice. The smell will go away before Mama Dukes gets home."

"You sure?"

"Positive. Gurl, next time you decide to be lazy and not iron these minions' clothes, you best make sure to check dem pockets before throwin' shit in the dryer. You're lucky that boy was only carryin' a dime bag, cuz an ounce would have really fuc..." he stopped himself, making Journey giggle. "Messed things up."

I scoffed out a chuckle.

"Besides, you got bigger problems than just some herb smellin' up in here. How old is the pothead again?"

"He just turned thirteen two weeks ago."

"Well, now you gonna havta deal with Cheech and him rollin' up doobies."

I inhaled a deep, steady breath. This was just another thing I had to face today.

What was I supposed to do with that? Tell Skyler? Have him hate me even more?

There was no right or wrong answers, either way you looked at it, I was screwed.

"I'm gonna get up outta here, my work is done for today. You're welcome. No need to walk me out, I might take a picture of Daddy Pierce to show my momma what her future grandkids might look like."

"Danté."

"Don't worry." He kept walking toward the door. "I'll take one for you too."

"Gah!" Journey chimed in.

"You want me to have a picture of your daddy?"

Her eyes widened, and I swear she winked at me.

"Don't worry! Doctor Daddy is probably fuckin' his fist to you already!"

"Danté! Language!"

"Pssst! Paris heard worse comin' out of her brother's mouths! Talk to you later, love ya!"

For the rest of the afternoon, I went about my normal routine. I cleaned up the rest of the house, made dinner, and got Journey ready for her third nap of the day, waiting on the brink of insanity for Jackson to get home, so I could confront him. Still not knowing what the hell I was going to say.

I wasn't equipped for the magnitude of the problem I was facing. This wasn't something I could have prepared or been ready for. There was no manual on how to handle a situation like this. I just had to go with my gut, my motherlike intuition, needing him to know this wasn't alright. He was too young to be smoking weed.

I took a deep, steady breath as I waited for him in his bedroom. My heart leapt out of my chest when I heard his footsteps down the hall. Secretly hoping this wasn't going to blow up in my face like everything else had with him.

The only other choice I had was to tell Skyler and let her handle it, but what would that say about me? I felt like this conversation at least needed to start between us.

The door swung open shortly after, and Jackson's stunned gaze connected with my concerned eyes. His caught off guard expression quickly fell to the bag of weed securely in my grasp.

He grinned. "I didn't know Mary Poppins got high. Is that why she's always so happy?"

"Very funny, Jackson. We both know this isn't mine."

"Are you trying to say it's mine?"

"Who else's would it be? It was in your jeans."

"It's not mine, and I have no idea how it got in there."

"Oh, so it just magically grew legs and jumped in your pocket without your knowledge? Just happened to show up while I placed them in the dryer to de-wrinkle your clothes? Try again."

He eyed me skeptically, throwing his backpack on his bed.

"What exactly are you trying to do here? Get me fired? Huh? That's quite the stunt to pull on me, even for you. Skyler could have me arrested! No more nursing school, no more future, no more nanny for you! No more nothing thanks to you. I'm already missing so many classes because I'm here caring for you instead of showing up for school!"

Offended, he put his hands up in the air. "Hey! I didn't know you were going to dry my jeans. That's on you."

"So, you did know the bag was in your jeans?"

He rolled his eyes and clenched his jaw. "No. I didn't."

"Then what? Huh? Explain to me what's going on here, before I explain to Skyler what I think is going on instead."

He arched an eyebrow, unfazed.

Jesus, does this kid feel anything?

Shrugging, he replied, "Then here's your chance to get back at me, Camila. Go tattle, I don't give a shit. Skyler's not my mother and neither are you."

I ignored his low blow. "So, you are smoking weed?"

"Why does it matter to you if I am?"

"You're only thirteen. You have your whole life ahead of you. You shouldn't be smoking weed that's why."

"And why is that, Mary Poppins? You're telling me you've never tried it?"

"Nice try. This isn't about me. This is about you."

"Actually, this is about both of us. You brought this on yourself. Stay out of my business and we won't have any problems. Yeah?"

"You know what? You're right about one thing, I'm not your mother, nor do I want to be. Why is it so hard for you to see that? The stunt you pulled today crossed the line, Jackson! This is not okay! You know Journey is with me all the time, and the house reeked of weed because of your ploy to get me fired! Thank God I found a surgical mask to put on her, or else I would have been beyond screwed! You put your baby sister's health in danger!"

"Oh bullshit, you're just being dramatic. There was barely any weed. She was fine."

"How would you know? Are you in medical school? Do you have a degree in—"

"Camila! What do you want from me? If you're looking for an apology, you're shit out of luck cuz you're not getting one."

Oh, hell no…

"Do you have any idea how hard I've worked to get to this point in my life? I didn't grow up like you with your million-dollar house, name brand clothes, and overly priced education that you take for granted." I pointed to myself, standing my ground. I wasn't leaving this room until I gave him a piece of my mind.

He needed to be put in his place, regardless of the consequences.

"I grew up poor with parents who struggled to put food on the table for all of their kids, but who still provided the best they could under the circumstances. I grew up with hand-me-downs, shopped at thrift stores, bought secondhand everything just so I could have shoes to wear, a book to read, a calculator to do my math homework with. I didn't grow up with a silver spoon in my mouth like you did! But I'll tell you one thing, Jackson, if I had, you bet your ass I would've appreciated it, and not have been a spoiled little shit like you who doesn't know the meaning of the word grateful."

His eyes glazed over. It was quick, but I saw it.

"It's not my fault your parents didn't know when to stop having kids."

My mouth dropped open. "Wow. There is no getting through to you, is there?"

"And yet, here you are, still trying."

I shook my head disappointed, stepping away from him. "I have nothing left to say to you."

"Great, cuz I don't want to hear anymore. Tell Skyler whatever you want, maybe it will make my dad come home for once."

I cocked my head to the side, the realization slapping me in the face.

Fast and hard.

"This wasn't about me at all, was it?"

"Get out of my room, Camila."

"You want me to rat you out, don't you?"

"I'm not going to say it again."

"Jackson, acting out isn't going to bring him hom—"

He got right in my face, seething, "Get out!" My feet stumbled as he backed me out of his room, forcing me into the hallway before slamming the door in my face.

"Jackson!" I banged on his door. "You can't do this! You can't just shut me out like this!"

"I just did!" he shouted through the door.

"Come on! Give me a chance! All I'm asking for is a chance!"

To my disbelief, he actually opened up. Getting right in my face again.

"What else do I have to do to—"

"What's going on here?" Skyler announced, breaking up our argument.

I turned to face her, still feeling Jackson's heated stare as I shoved the bag of weed in my back pocket.

Still unsure of what to do.

He watched my every move, waiting for the other shoe to drop.

"Yeah, Camila, what's going on here?" Jackson baited.

Was he testing me?

"I- I- I- I mean ... we were just..."

There were so many ways this could go down. I could tell Skyler and then what?

What would that solve?

What would that help?

The more I thought about it, the more I realized Jackson was the All-Star quarterback for his school. Football was his life, and I don't think he'd risk that for anything.

It was the only thing he truly seemed passionate about, other than making my life a living, breathing hell of course.

It didn't make sense. He wouldn't throw that all away for some hits off a joint. There wasn't even enough in the bag for him to roll one up. Jackson wanted his dad home, even if it meant he had to pay the price to make it happen.

My heart hurt more for him in that moment, than it did all the other times he pushed me away, combined.

I opened my mouth to say something but quickly shut it, looking over at Jackson. We weren't more than a foot apart, but it felt like miles of distance were placed between us.

Physically and mentally.

There was so much confusion evident on his face, and I felt it deep within my being. We could have been standing there for a minute or an hour. Time seemed to standstill, but the pain seemed to keep going on all around me.

I locked eyes with Skyler, muttering, "Jackson and I were just arguing about his laundry habits."

I felt him stiffen beside me.

"Jackson knows how to do laundry?"

"Or lack thereof," I added, smiling over at him.

He narrowed his eyes at me, more confused than ever before. But for the first time since I started working here two months ago, I saw vulnerability run through his eyes. It may have only been for a few seconds, though, it was enough to know I was doing the right thing.

Jackson wasn't as strong as he pretended to be. Deep down he was just as lost as his father, maybe?

We may have come from two different worlds, but for a few moments that afternoon, we finally reached middle ground. Who knows how long we'd stay there, all I knew was I wouldn't go down without a fight.

Even if it meant standing on Jackson's side.

Something or someone needed to bring their father home.

Even if that something or someone...

Was *me*.

Fifteen

AIDEN
Then: Sixteen-years-old

"What would you say if I kissed you right now?" I whispered against Bailey's neck.

"I'd say what took you so long."

This was by far the best part of her being my girl. I was able to kiss her anytime I wanted.

I skimmed my lips along her pouty mouth, murmuring, "Do you like that?"

"Aiden," she panted, molding herself into my chest. My warm breath ignited her cool skin in a frenzy of shivers as I continued to tease my way from ear to ear. Lightly pecking along her jawline till a moan escaped her mouth, *"Yes, right there."*

She was sitting on my desk, and I was standing in between her long legs. My hands roaming up and down her bare thighs, kneading, squeezing, and bringing her ass closer to the edge of the old tarnished wood.

We were in my room on a Saturday night, supposedly studying, but there wasn't much of that going on. Our books were scattered around my room, note cards sprawled across the worn carpet, notebooks flung onto my small twin bed in the corner. Next to the other two beds that occupied the rest of the space.

My foster assholes were gone for the night to who the fuck knows where. And the three kids I shared a room with were sleeping over at friends' houses.

All that mattered was we were alone, and Bailey was in my arms.

My nose skated up the side of her neck, inhaling the scent of her sunflower perfume. She smelled like everything I ever wanted.

"My foster family took in a new kid," she said out of nowhere. Trying to get her mind to think straight, and not let it wander to what she wanted me to do with my hands.

We'd never gone further than kissing, but I swear something felt different about tonight.

I grinned. "Does he smell like a butthole?"

She turned ten shades of red. "Oh my God, Aiden." She tried to push me away, I didn't move an inch. "You're never going to let me live that down, are you?"

"Never." I smiled, kissing her luscious lips.

"I was a mess."

"You were adorable."

"You always say that."

"I only speak the truth."

She rolled her eyes, smiling. "I thought you were going to kiss me."

"Where do you want my mouth, Bailey? Here?" I pecked her lips, softly grazing my mouth down to her cleavage. "Here?" Never taking my eyes off her heated stare, I slowly got down on my knees, groaning, "Or here?" Licking my lips, I nodded to her pussy.

Her breath hitched and her legs locked up.

"Do you trust me?"

"With my life."

I smiled, biting my lower lip. "I can make you feel good, Bay. Really, really good."

"Oh yeah? Where'd you learn how to do that?"

"A man never reveals his secrets."

"Oh! Is there a man in this room?" she mocked, and I bit the inside of her thigh. "Ouch!"

"Be a good girl, or you don't get a happy ending."

"I don't want a happy ending. I want a happily ever after. With two sons named Jackson and Jagger who look exactly like their daddy."

I kissed the spot where I had just bit her, gradually making my way up her leg. "Is that right?"

"Mmm hmm…"

"Seems like you've given this a lot of thought, Bailey Button, not to be confused with Belly Button."

"Are you trying to make me cry?"

"No, I'm trying to make you wet. Is it working?"

She giggled. "Maybe you should see for yourself, Aiden Pierce."

"Are you testing me, baby? Cuz you know I want nothing more than to bury my face inside of your panties right now."

Her mouth dropped open. "Where did you learn to talk like this?"

"Why? You like it?"

She cleared her throat. "Maybe."

"Good," I rasped. "Spread your legs further for me then."

She did, shaking a little. Anticipating what I had in store for her.

"Jackson and Jagger, huh? Sounds like you want a country band."

"Maybe I do. You'd look so cute wearing a cowboy hat."

I spread her legs wider, continuing my way up her inner thigh.

In the best Southern accent I could muster, I replied, "Now I reckon that means we'd need a little girl who looks just like her momma, and by that, I mean *you*."

"A little girl? Then I'd have to share my thunder."

"A king needs a princess as much as he needs a queen."

She beamed, her heart of gold melting in the palm of my hand with each word that left my tongue. I stared deep into her eyes. "Promise me you'll give me a baby girl who we will name Journey."

"Jackson, Jagger, and Journey? Now that sounds like a country band if I ever heard one."

With a serious expression, I stated the truth, "We have a long road ahead of us, baby, but it will always be worth the journey. Because at the end of the day, it's what leads us back to each other."

Her eyes watered and her lip trembled.

"Promise me, Bailey."

"I promise." She wiped away a tear.

"Happy tears, right?"

She nodded. "How do you do that, Aiden? How can you look at me like that?"

"Like what?"

"Like I'm your whole world."

"It's easy. You are," I simply stated, meaning each and every word.

She shut her eyes, the emotion too much for her to handle. I slowly stood up and pulled her toward me, wrapping her legs around my waist. Pressing my forehead up against her, I reached up and swept the hair away from her face.

"Look at me, Bay."

She cautiously did.

Her bright blue eyes were my undoing. The sincerity in them did it to me every damn time.

So much emotion erupted behind her gaze, and I knew it mirrored mine. There was no need for words, our eyes spoke for themselves as my hands caressed the sides of her cheeks. Without any hesitation, I tugged her mouth toward mine. Softly breathing inches away from her heated face. Taking in the curve of her eyes, the light freckles from the sun, and the way her perfect skin felt along my fingertips. Before our mouths became one.

Her lips were just as I remembered, even though I had claimed her mouth hundreds of times by that point. It always felt like I was coming home.

Bailey would forever be my home.

She sought out my tongue before I had the opportunity to find hers. Moaning into my mouth the second our tongues collided.

Our mouths went to war with one another. The kiss was soft but demanding, controlled but passionate, and fucking intense as all hell.

"Aiden," she erratically breathed, panting on my lips.

"Yeah, baby?" I growled with the same heady tone.

"I want you."

My thoughts.

My words.

They were all suddenly tangled with one another.

"I want you more than I have ever wanted anyone in my entire life," I confessed.

She whimpered, begging, "Please."

It was as clear as day.

My eyes glazed over.

My jaw clenched.

My body tensed.

Like a possessed man.

My cock got hard as fuck.

"You're so beautiful, Bailey. So fucking beautiful," I whispered, kissing down the side of her neck. Inch by inch down to her breasts, leaving a trail of desire in my wake.

Lapping.

Needing.

Sucking.

She became my undoing.

In one quick movement, her dress and bra were off, and all she was left in was her panties. The vision of her topless in front of me was a memory I'd take to my grave.

I sucked her nipple into my mouth for the first time ever, and I wasn't just referring to hers. Bailey was my first everything.

Her friendship.

Her lips.

Her love.

Her pussy would eventually be mine and only mine as well.

She squirmed beneath my touch as my left hand caressed her other breast. She felt me everywhere, every inch of her skin tingling from the sensations of my mouth and hands.

She could feel my hard dick, pressing on her wet core through the thin fabric of my athletic shorts. Purposely moving my hips to create friction that sent shivers all over our bodies.

Peering up at her with hooded eyes, I broke the silence, "I want to taste you, Bay. I want to make you come in my mouth."

I didn't know what the hell I was doing, but I'd watched enough porn to figure it out. I wanted this to be good for my girl, she deserved that and so much more.

Bailey moaned in response, sucking in her bottom lip. Reeling in our passion, her back arched for me to do exactly what I wanted.

In another swift movement, I was back down on my knees, sliding her panties off her legs, and throwing them to the side. Inhaling Bailey's sweet, intoxicating scent.

"Fuck..." I breathed out before taking her clit into my mouth. Sucking in a forceful yet tender back and forth motion.

I had never felt anything like it before.

Her breath became heavy…

Her chest rose and fell…

Her legs started to shake…

Until she couldn't keep her eyes open any longer.

As soon as she felt my fingers at her opening, she locked eyes with me again.

"I won't take your virginity with my fingers, but one day I will with my cock."

Her eyes widened and her breath hitched.

"Let me feel you from the inside, Bay. Just so I know what it feels like to be home."

She nodded, giving me the okay.

"Jesus Christ, Bailey. You're so fucking tight, you're going to make me come."

"Well that makes two of us."

The way my mouth devoured her, and my fingers explored her, it was too much to handle. She couldn't take it anymore. Her pussy got wetter and wetter.

She exhaled.

She panted.

She clenched.

I watched.

I tasted.

I made love to her with my mouth.

"You like that, Bay?"

"Yes," she shamelessly moaned, leaning her head back and falling apart again.

"Like that?" I sucked her harder. "Or like this?" I sucked her longer.

"Ah…" was all she could say, grabbing ahold of my hair.

"Move your hips, Bay. Ride my face," I demanded, wanting to come as bad as she did.

"Oh, God … oh, Aiden…"

"Let go, baby. Just let go for me."

And holy fuck, she did.

A growl escaped from deep within my chest, vibrating against her core. Both of us coming at the exact same time. I didn't touch myself once but having Bailey at my mercy was an orgasm I had no control over.

She gasped, sucking in air, almost falling over the edge. I sat up, catching her lips with my mouth. Making us into one person.

She instantly reached for the elastic band of my gym shorts.

"No," I rasped, stopping her hand.

"What?" she asked, taken back, trying to catch her breath.

I kissed the tip of her nose, looking deep into her eyes once again and said,

"Not here. Not now. You deserve better than this shithole. When you come from my cock, I want it to be the most romantic fucking thing you ever experience."

And it would be.

I'd   make   sure   of   it.

Sixteen

Camila

Now

I refused to go on like this.

"Journey, how did my favorite water get in here?" I asked, holding up the Hint bottle I pulled out of the fridge. A serious expression quickly took over my face, baffled by how this kept happening. "There's no way this exact brand would be in here. I just told you about it yesterday."

She babbled at me from her play saucer, answering my question I was sure.

"This makes absolutely no sense. At first, I believed this could be a coincidence that the stuff I shared with you just keeps showing up, but there's no way I believe that now. I'm not going crazy. You can't talk."

"Gah!"

"I'm sorry that was rude, but you know what I mean, Little Miss."

"Bah!"

I grabbed her from the saucer and took her into the living room. "Journey, what's going on?" I questioned, gazing around the big open space, setting her down on the floor with some toys. "Are there cameras all around? Is someone watching us?"

"Gah!"

"Ugh!" I replied frustrated. "That's it, I'm going in, Journey." I pulled my hair up, tying it in a high bun on the top of my head. "You're no help."

"Lah!"

"I know you resent that." I moved my way around the room, searching all the shelves, the TV stand cubbies, and book case in the corner of the room.

Nothing.

I kept coming up empty.

"I've been here for three months! There's no way I wouldn't have seen a camera by now."

Before I lost it completely and started throwing random stuff across the room in hopes of it breaking and a camera falling out, I walked back to Journey. Looking at the array of toys and stuffed animals surrounding her, when my eyes landed on one in particular. I reached for her bunny off the floor and glared at it. The fluffy white fur ball was judging me.

I looked straight into its beady eyes. "Are you a camera? Can you see me? Because if you can, it's really not cool that no one has told me there are cameras in this house. Not that I've done anything wrong, but still, I deserve to know if I'm being watched. I'd like to think I've earned your trust."

Now I was getting pissed.

Really pissed.

Thinking about all the times I'd been with Journey, when it should have been her parents. All the times I dealt with Jackson, who'd only became a bigger pain in my ass in the last month. Not to mention Jagger, who didn't speak at all.

I cleaned up after them.

I took care of them as if they were my own.

Put their needs above all else.

I'd been working sixty and seventy-hour weeks. Missing classes because most of the time I'd never make it home, staying in the guest bedroom instead. Curtis hadn't seen me in who knows how long, I hoped he was okay.

Skyler was too pregnant to move, let alone handle the hell raisers who didn't appreciate a damn thing in life. I was exhausted.

Beyond exhausted.

Now to learn there were cameras watching me…

Well that, *that* was just fucking bullshit.

So, I did what any woman would have done in my position, I let the bunny in my hands have it.

"Do you have any idea how tired I am? No, you don't because you're not here! You're with your patients who are obviously more important to you than the children you've brought into this world!"

"Gah!"

I pointed the stuffed animal at her. "You tell him, Journey!"

She kicked her chubby legs, her face turning bright red. "Gah! Lah! Bah! Gah!"

I turned it back to me. "Exactly what she said! She needs you! Not me! YOU! So instead of recording my time with her to make sure she's safe and taken care of, how about you actually do it yourself from time to time? I understand you're trying to provide for them, but I haven't met or seen you once! Not one time in three months! Do you have any idea how weird that is?! I report to Skyler, a woman who's not even blood related to these kids, when it should be you. Where are you?!"

I spun the bunny around and unzipped the back, adamantly thinking there was a camera inside, and I was going to find it once and for all. I pulled out all the stuffing, throwing the fluff everywhere.

Seething, "Can you hear me? I'm going to find you! And then we're really going to have words!"

"You know that's a stuffed animal, right?"

I jumped as soon as I heard Jackson's voice, abruptly spinning to face him. I shouted, "No! It's your dad!"

"Since when did my dad become a bunny's ass?"

"He's in here! I know it!"

He cocked his head to the side, narrowing his eyes at me. "Mary Poppins, Journey is watching you lose your mind on one of her favorite stuffed animals. So, before you traumatize her any more than you already have, put it down and step away from the bunny."

I scowled, stepping toward him. Shoving the stuffed animal into his chest. "Fine. Then I'm going to find the man that's inside the bunny."

"This isn't *Toy Story*, Camila. There's no one inside of it."

"You'll see," I roared, making my way toward the garage door.

"Where are you going?!"

"I just told you!"

I sidestepped Jagger, who was standing in the kitchen with a huge grin on his face as if he knew exactly what I was talking about.

"What about Journey?"

"You can watch her!"

"What? I've never watched her before! You can't just leave her with me! It's not my job to watch her, it's yours!"

"You can handle it for an hour! Just hold her, feed her, change her diaper! You've seen me do it hundreds of times!"

"Mary Poppins, what the fu—"

"Finish that sentence, and I'll wash your mouth out with soap when I get back!" I slammed the door behind me, grabbed the car keys off the holder, and stepped into the vehicle I was only allowed to use for the kids.

I couldn't think of a better time to use it more than now. Their father was going to hear what I had to say, with or without his consent. He needed to be here, he was missing everything, and I loved Journey too much to allow things to continue as they had been. But it wasn't just for Journey, I cared for them all. Even the biggest pain in my ass.

My thoughts weighed heavy on my mind as I drove toward the hospital, thinking only of his kids. Not caring how it would make me look in their father's eyes. I was doing this for them.

What should have taken minutes, felt like hours before I was barreling through the surgical unit doors to the nurse's station.

"Hi, I'm looking for Dr. Pierce. I'm—"

"Camila, his nanny."

I jerked back, completely caught off guard.

How did she know me?

"I'm Renee, his RN."

Oh, it must be through Skyler, since I had to take that CPR certification. She must recognize my face from my driver's license.

"Are you okay?"

"What?" I shook away the thoughts. "I'm fine. Do you know where I can find him?"

She looked at the computer screen in front of her. "Oh, you're in luck. He just finished his rounds. He should be in his office." She nodded down the hall. "Go past those double doors towards the elevator and then take it up to the fifth floor. His office is 519."

"Alright, thank you."

"Does he know you're coming?"

I shook my head no and she slowly nodded with an inquisitive look in her eyes.

"Do you think it's best to meet him here?"

"How do you know we—"

"Journey is adorable, isn't she? She's gotten so big. You're amazing with her. A real natural."

"How do you—"

"I know Aiden appreciates it."

"How does he—"

"Camila, I wouldn't ask questions you already know the answer to."

I swallowed hard. Our eyes lingered on one another for a few more seconds before I stepped away from the desk. Breaking our profound stare, I put one foot in front of the other, striding toward the elevator she just directed me to.

I was so confused...

Dr. Pierce didn't know me, had never met me. He wouldn't be the one talking about me, would he? There has to be cameras in the house, no way there couldn't be.

My thoughts ran wild through my frazzled mind, embarking on a course of their own. It didn't help that Renee's penetrating gaze lingered on me until the doors of the elevator closed behind me.

As a result of what could only be explained as one of the most eluding conversations I'd ever had, the wind in my sails deflated a little, but I didn't allow the minor setback to deter my mission on getting through to Dr. Pierce about his kids. The only difference now, I wasn't as pissed off as I was when I initially walked through the doors of the hospital.

Which was probably a good thing.

What was going on?

I hated being out of control of my own emotions. No good would ever come of it. I knew from experience. There wasn't a worse feeling in the world than having your mind governed by someone you didn't even know. Someone you'd never even personally met.

I needed my voice to be heard, but why did that seem so much harder now?

So much more real.

The moment the elevator pinged on the fifth floor, I stepped off into a quiet hallway and instantly felt it. There was a strong shift in the air, the space, the energy all around me. This strong force steering me, guiding me, taking over my heart.

My mind.

My soul.

Every inch of my skin stirred with an awakening I'd never experienced before. It was surreal, breathing new life into my being.

Something was brewing inside of me, something immense.

Significant.

Life-altering.

The more I tried to make sense of it, the less it did. My breathing hitched, my pulse quickened, and my heart started beating out of my chest. I didn't move, too afraid if I did the emotions would leave me as well. I closed my eyes and took a deep breath in through my nose and out through my mouth, waiting for I don't know what. Getting lost in the overwhelming senses that were yanking me along for the ride.

I licked my lips, my mouth suddenly dry. This unexplainable urge seized up in my chest, and heat surged through my veins.

Pulling.

Dragging.

Taking me hostage.

My feet began to move, and my body followed as I opened my eyes. Consumed with the electricity that sparked internally, igniting a fire, burning all reasoning down to the ground.

Almost instantly, I was engulfed in a masculine scent that drove all my nerve endings into high alert. Like gas to a flame, I exploded.

Erupted.

A hot blaze seared into my flesh, and just like that I felt it again.

Except this time there was no mistaking it, there wasn't an *it*.

The *it* was a him.

All along, I felt him.

Dr. Pierce.

Aiden.

Seventeen

Camila

Now

I softly gasped at the sight of the man standing near the nurse's station in front of me. My view obstructed by a supply cart, I could see him, but he couldn't see me. I just stood there unknowingly, glaring at him without even realizing I was doing so.

"What the hell is happening?" I murmured to myself.

I never imagined I could feel this way about a stranger. A man who up until this moment, I thought may have been a figment of my imagination. I lost countless hours, days, months to the endless questions of who he was, where he was, and what was wrong with him.

And there he was in the flesh.

Dressed in blue scrubs and a white lab coat with a stethoscope wrapped around his collar. Emphasizing the three cross tattoos on his neck. My eyes were drawn to them, searching for the story I knew that caliber of ink held.

He was tall. Way taller than my five-feet-four frame. He'd tower over me, and that thought alone sent shivers coursing down my spine just thinking of his dominance. But with that emotion came shame.

"Camila, he's married," I whispered out loud, needing to remind myself.

But is he?
Where is she?
Where is his wife?

My captivated stare shifted toward his ring finger, and sure enough proudly on display was his wedding band. A sick effect settled in my stomach.

How could I have this intense response for my married employer?

I wasn't this woman. I would NEVER be this woman. Although, it was so much more than that.

He was so much more than that.

As was everything I was enduring.

I didn't understand any of it, looking at the man I'd never met in awe. Words couldn't describe how handsome he was in person. His piercing blue eyes were as bright as crystal blue water. His salt-and-pepper beard appeared as if he hadn't shaved in months. He appeared as exhausted as I felt, like he hadn't slept in who knows how long. But that wasn't what caught my attention the most, it was the sadness distorting his expression, the detachment in his gaze, the despair radiating all around him.

There was this certain vulnerability to him that I felt in the space between us. However, just as quick as it emerged, it was gone. Whatever it was had me questioning what I believed about him in the first place. The emotional attachment I felt for a man I had only just encountered was as overpowering and controlling as everything else had been up until this point. I couldn't tear my eyes away from him, which only made me even more confused.

More cautious.

More curious about him.

In that place and time, all I craved was to see him smile. To catch a glimpse of the man I'd only stared at in photos. He seemed as though he was a walking paradox of contradictions. I was seeing the side of him that everyone saw, but there was something else under his allure.

All I knew was, I liked it.

I wanted more.

I needed more.

The uncomfortable silence hammered all around me, tearing into my insecurities that this was a bad idea. I shouldn't be in this hospital. I shouldn't be feeling anything for him other than what I was supposed to. Only adding to my plaguing emotions.

He was my employer, nothing else but that.

Right as I took a step in his direction, longing to hear his answers to my relentless questions, I heard him snap, "What the fuck is this?" in a sharp masculine tone, stopping my descent forward.

It was only then I realized there was a woman standing in front of him. Her stunned appearance mirrored mine.

"Why were these patients' charts on my desk?"

"Dr. Pierce, I thought—"

"I don't pay you to give me your thoughts, Miranda. I pay you to do your goddamn job. If filing these patient's charts is too hard for you, you shouldn't be working in my hospital."

I jolted back as did she, never expecting him to say that.

What an asshole.

"Dr. Pierce, I was just doing—"

"Doing what, wasting my time?"

"No, that's not—"

"I don't have the time to do your job and mine. Last I checked I have MD after my name, I save people's lives. This is my life and you're fucking it up by being incompetent. It's simple, all I ask is for you to file the charts, stay out of my way, and do the job you were hired to do. Now, are you capable of that?"

She nodded, practically in tears. "Yes, Dr. Pierce."

"Good, now repeat after me... I will not try to help in any other way but doing my job. If I can't do that, because I don't know how to follow protocol, then I will get fired and become someone else's incompetent pain in the ass." He looked down, writing something in the chart in front of him.

"But, Dr. Pierce, if you could just let me explain—"

"For Christ's sake!" He slammed the chart shut and threw a pen onto the counter, making both of us jump back. "There is nothing that could explain why I walked into my office to find a stack of charts on my desk that should have already been filed."

"I-I-I—"

"Don't start with the tears. I don't have time for that either. Do your job, or I'll find someone who can." He abruptly threw the charts at her, making her scramble to catch them before they hit the floor.

My mouth dropped open, and just as I was about to intervene, his RN did for me.

"Aiden!" she chided, walking up to him.

"Don't start, Renee. I don't have time for your bullshit either."

She nodded to the woman with a look of gratitude to walk away, and she did exactly that.

Renee turned to glare at him, like this wasn't the first time she'd done so. "You need a break. You haven't slept in two days. You've been on call for longer than that. And don't get me started on the last time you ate. You can't go on like this, Aiden. It's not healthy or fair to anyone, including your patients. Remember the time when everyone used to mean something to you?"

I narrowed my eyes, contemplating what she had just said.

It wasn't just his kids he was neglecting?

"Bailey wouldn't have wanted this for you."

His fists connected with the counter, not startling her in the least. "Don't you ever say her name to me again. Do you understand me?" He eyed her up and down, backing away in the opposite direction of me. Quickly spewing, "I'm the doctor, you're the nurse, Renee, know your role in *my* hospital."

My eyes widened as did hers.

Before she could reply, he spun and walked away, leaving us both there shocked and dismayed.

"Wow," I blurted too loud, causing her eyes to connect with mine. "I-I-I-yo-yo-yo..." I immediately started stuttering, unable to form words. My tongue getting twisted with my Spanish dialect.

"I'm so sorry you had to see that." She deeply sighed, embarrassed. Shaking her head for me. "He wasn't always like this. I know how that sounds after what you've just witnessed, but trust me ... he was the kindest, sweetest doctor, *man* you'd ever meet. I won't make excuses for him, but circumstances change people. The hospital knows what he's going through since his wife—"

"Code blue! Code blue! All available medical staff to room 521-bed A. I repeat, we have a code blue in room 521-bed A," the speakers in the hallway went off. "Shit! I have to go. It was nice to meet you, Camila," she concluded, running off in the same direction as Dr. Pierce.

Without giving it any thought, I went after him. My feet moved on their own, not walking but running this time. Going straight toward his office.

I ran faster.

Harder.

And with more determination.

My feet burned against the tile floor with each stride and sentiment bulldozing its way through my head. My heart pounded, my ears rang, and my vigorous breathing escalated higher and louder with every second that passed. The adrenaline flowing through my bloodstream had already taken over.

He was getting a piece of my mind.

No matter what.

I rounded the corner, coming face to face with his office door that was slightly ajar. I saw him sitting at his desk, his body hunched over with his head in between his hands and once again it stopped me dead in my tracks. The heavy weight of what was devouring him alive had me frozen in place.

He was in a trancelike state, lost in what could only be described as his own personal Hell.

My stomach fluttered, my heart dropped. I was living in, breathing in, settled in his turmoil, becoming one with all his emotions. Watching the good doctor breakdown in front of me was a vision I'd never forget. His body took on a whole different demeanor. The cold, calloused bastard was gone, and a broken man sat in his place, not holding anything back.

Tears rolled down his face, and a desperate heave escaped his chest.

I leaned against the doorframe for support, witnessing his mind and heart going to war with one another. He didn't stop, and I wondered if he could feel me too. Knowing it was a stupid thought, but it was there, nonetheless.

His rage quickly took over, replacing what felt like the hole in his chest. I blinked, and he grabbed the picture frame he must have been lost in, forcefully chucking it across the room.

Roaring, "Motherfucker!"

I hesitated, nothing more, nothing less.

He stood up so fast, his leather chair slammed into the bookcase behind him. If I didn't know any better, I'd have thought he was coming after me when his feet started stomping on the ground, hauling ass out of his office. I turned, hiding behind the door. This wasn't the right time to confront him, and I was beginning to think there would never be one.

As soon as I heard him trampling his way down the hall away from his office, my cellphone rang. Skyler's name lit up my screen, and panic rapidly took over my senses.

Going from one fucked up situation to the next.

"Oh my God, I'm so sorry I left Jackson with Jour—"

"No need to apologize, Camila, I understand. I would have done the same thing had a family member needed me."

"A family member?"

"Yeah, Jackson told me your mom fell down the stairs, and you had to rush her to the emergency room. He said he told you to take the car, so you wouldn't have to wait for the bus. I get it. Not a problem at all."

My eyes widened. "Right. I still should have called and told you, though," I replied on autopilot.

"Is she alright?"

"Uh huh."

"That's great to hear."

"It is."

"When family is involved, we lose our minds. Besides, it did Jackson some good to watch his baby sister. He was actually dancing with her like you do when I walked into the house," she chuckled.

"He was?"

"Yes. Don't tell him I told you, but I think he's starting to come around to you."

"Yeah, I guess so."

"Anyway, I won't keep you. Will you be back tomorrow, or do you need a few days to tend to your mom?"

"I'll be back tomorrow."

"Sounds good. Have a good night, Camila."

"You too."

She hung up.

It was only then that I realized I was standing in Dr. Pierce's office. I don't know what blew me away more.

The fact that Jackson covered for me or that the picture his father threw across the room was one of him and his wife…

On their wedding day.

Eighteen

AIDEN
Then: Seventeen-years-old

"Bailey," I warned as she kissed along the side of my neck. "We're not doing this."

"Aiden..." She slowly pecked her way down my body. "Please. We've waited so long."

"Bay, the other kids are right outside the door and so are my foster parents."

"Actually, Mario got called into work, and the only kid here is Everly."

"That still leaves Eva."

She gazed up at me through her long lashes, smirking like a fool. "Your foster mom is in her room on the other side of the house. She's too pregnant with a baby of her own to move. Besides, I locked the door."

"I refuse to disrespect them in any way, Bay. Not after everything they've done for me. For *us*."

I spoke nothing but the truth. This was the first family I'd been placed with who was worth a damn. At first, when my umpteenth caseworker assigned me to them a little less than a year ago, I didn't believe it, but they proved themselves more times than I could count. It was as insignificant as meals on the table several times a day, where everyone talked about the peak of their day.

To them always taking an interest in their foster kids doing their homework, studying for exams, just making sure we were ready for the school day ahead. Eva would pack lunches, take and pick up everyone from school on time, while Mario went to work. We were made a priority for once.

My fondest memory was when Mario helped me restore my 1964 Chevelle I found in an old junkyard nearby. She was still a work in progress, but we were able to get her started and drivable. I was lucky he knew some mechanics in the neighborhood who found used parts we needed dirt cheap. We'd spent months working on rebuilding her engine and replacing her tires, when the day finally came to get her to start.

"Okay, Aiden, start her up!" Mario hollered from under the hood.

I sat in the driver's seat and pushed in the clutch with my left foot, turning over the ignition.

Putt, putt, putt.

"Give her some gas!"

I tried again, this time pressing my right foot on the gas and sure enough she rumbled to life.

"You hear that, Mario?! My girl can purr!"

He laughed, shutting the hood to walk over to me. "How's it feel?"

"Like she was made just for me."

I'd wanted a hotrod for as long as I could remember. One day, I'd have a garage full of them. This was one of the many accomplishments I set for myself.

He patted my back, gripping onto my shoulder. "You did it, son. I'm so proud of you."

This wasn't the first time he'd said he was proud of me, but the more I heard it, the easier it was to believe.

I wrapped my arm around his shoulder, emphasizing, "We did it."

Our dynamic was very much of a father and son. He knew I never had a dad, or a good example of an honorable man in my life, so he tried the best he could to provide that for me. Mario set the bar high, knowing it was what I needed without me ever having to ask. He spent weeks teaching me how to drive, going through how to shift and which gear was which. How to parallel park, so I could get my license and wouldn't have to rely on the city bus to take me to and from work after school anymore.

Every free second I had, when I wasn't with Bailey, was spent helping Mario and Eva with my foster siblings. It was the least I could do for all they provided. From clean clothes, to toothbrushes, to beds with clean sheets and a pillow, and so much more.

The list went on with their generosity and love. I know it may seem trivial to most people, but for two kids who grew up in the shitty ass system, it meant the world to us. Bailey wasn't even their assigned foster child and they took care of her as well, knowing she meant everything to me.

These two human beings had hearts of gold, a blessing to many, taking in kid after kid with no questions asked. For the first time in my life, I felt like I had a real home, a family who loved me as much as I did them.

"Baby, this can't be how you imagined making love for the first time?"

She sighed. "No, you're right."

"I always am."

She rolled her eyes, hiding back a smile.

"I know it's hard, I'm just too irresistible. It's a curse really."

"Is that right?"

"It's the price I have to pay for having a huge cock."

She busted out laughing. I loved making her laugh.

"I want to call your bullshit, but I can't. Not that I've seen others or anything. I mean, you've probably seen them in the locker room. You tell me, are other guys as huge as you?"

"Bailey, my cock is the only one you'll ever see. End of story."

"What kind of answer is that?"

"The only one that matters."

She giggled. "I love it when you act all alpha and possessive."

With a serious expression, I stated, "Who's acting?"

"You'll always be the only guy I'll ever want."

"You don't have to want me, Bay, cuz I'll always be right here. With you."

"How do you always say the right things?"

"I only know how to speak the truth. My word is all I have." I eyed her with a predatory regard. "But since your face is already down there, you can suck my cock."

"Oh, can I now?"

149

I nodded, grinning.

"I thought you said we weren't doing this."

"I said we weren't making love. My dick in your mouth is always fair game, Beauty. What kind of man would I be if I didn't give my girl what she wanted, especially when she's begging me for it?"

"You cocky asshole," she teased.

"And you can't get enough of it."

I was about to grip the back of her neck when we heard Everly shout, "Aiden!" through the door. "Mommy peed herself! She peed herself! She gets no M&M's!"

We laughed. Bailey chuckling, "What's that all about?"

"Who knows with Everly."

She was two and a half going on twenty-one. The family was potty training her and every time she used the bathroom, she got her favorite M&M's.

I walked toward the door, unlocked it and opened it to a little girl who was butt-ass naked.

"What are you doing?"

"Momma's naked. Me naked too."

"What? Where—"

She giggled, taking off toward Eva's bedroom. Bailey and I quickly followed, knocking on the open door.

"Ahhhh!" Eva screamed out in pain.

"Bailey, go in there and see what's going on please."

She hastily nodded, calling out, "Eva, I'm coming in!"

"Ahhhh!" she yelled again.

"Oh my God! Eva, are you in labor?"

"Yes!"

"Aiden, call 9-1-1!" Bailey ordered. "She needs an ambulance!"

I ran into the living room to grab the house phone.

"9-1-1, what's your emergency?"

"It's Eva... she's uh... she's having a baby," I stuttered, trying to keep my cool.

"Okay, sir, stay calm. Where is she now?"

"In her bathroom."

"Is her bag of water intact?"

I nervously paced back and forth. "Her what?"

"Has her water broke, sir?"

"I don't know, yes, she peed..."

Everly enthusiastically nodded, skipping around. "Yes, Momma peed in her pants! She gets no M&M's, der all mine cuz I pooped in da potty!"

"What's your name?"

"Aiden."

"Okay Aiden, I need you to time her contractions. Can you do that for me?"

"Yeah, I can do that. Give me a minute." I grabbed the bag of M&M's off the counter and Everly's eyes lit up. "I'm going to turn on your movie and you're going to sit on the couch and eat your chocolate like a good girl, okay?"

"Beauty and da Beast!" she beamed, already going to town on the bag of candy. Everly loved that Disney movie, always claiming it was Bailey on the screen, and I couldn't agree more. She looked just like the make-believe character. It was why I started calling her Beauty, named after the heroine, Belle.

After I helped Everly get dressed, I made my way back toward Eva's bedroom, announcing, "Eva! I need to come in and help!"

"Come in! I wrapped a towel around her!" Bailey responded for her from what sounded like the shower. Her voice echoed in the air.

"Why are you in the shower?" I asked when I saw where they were.

I hit the speaker button on the phone to free up my hands and reassure Eva help was on the way.

"Eva was trying to clean herself up after her water broke."

"So, it was her water?" the operator questioned.

Eva nodded, breathing in and out. Focusing on Bailey sitting in front of her.

"Yes," I told the operator.

"Okay, the EMS is en route. How far are her contractions?"

Eva blurted in a heavy tone, "Contractions are a minute apart," breathing through the agony. "Baby is coming. She's coming right now!"

"Okay, I need everyone to stay calm. The EMS might not make it in time with how close those contractions are happening, Ma'am."

"What?!" They screamed in unison, while I stayed calm for everyone including myself.

"You may need to deliver this baby, but don't worry I will walk you through it."

"I need to push!" Eva stated, bearing down.

"She needs to push, Aiden!"

"I have ears, Bay!"

"I need someone to look and see if the baby's head is crowning."

Bailey and I locked eyes, and I nodded over to Eva.

"Oh man." Her eyes widened. "I don't know if I can do this, Aiden. I don't like blood. I get queasy when I get a papercut."

"I know, but you have to."

"Aiden, I can't. I just can't do it!"

"Someone has to do it," the operator spoke up. "Or the baby could go into distress."

Before I gave it any thought, I asked, "Eva, is it alright if I look?" Wanting to be respectful.

It wasn't like I had much of a choice in the situation. Either I did this, or I'd be risking two lives, Eva's and the baby. I couldn't live with myself if something happened to them. Being the one to deliver their baby girl was the ultimate way to show my appreciation for all they did.

A way to show my gratitude for everything they'd done for me.

For us.

"Yes! Please! Get this baby out of me NOW!"

Bailey scooted out of the way to sit up by Eva's head, supporting it in her lap, while I sat in between her legs. Mentally preparing myself for I don't know what.

"Ahh! I can't hold her in any longer! I'm pushing! I'm pushing!" she panted, squeezing onto Bailey's hand as excruciating pain ripped through her body.

"Holy shit," I breathed out, looking at baby girl's head coming out. "Yeah, she's crowning!"

"Okay, just a few more pushes, Eva. I need you to bear down as soon as the next wave of contractions hit. Hold it for a count of ten then breathe. Deep breathes in and out after. Just remember to breathe, your baby will be here before you know it," the woman on the phone instructed. "Aiden, once you see the baby's shoulders, it will get a lot easier," she informed. "I need you to grab a towel and get ready to catch the baby."

I nodded as if she could see me, amazed at what was happening in front of my eyes. I reached behind me to pull the towel off the rack.

"Aiden, can you hear me?"

"Yes, but I've… I've never held a baby."

"It's not hard. Just make sure you support the head, alright?"

"Okay."

I'd never been so nervous, watching a new life come into this world. My hands shook as I reached for the baby girl, supporting her neck and head, careful not to hurt her.

"Alright, Eva, only a few more pushes and you will get to meet your baby," I assured, the panic quickly subsiding.

"You are doing amazing, Eva. Whenever you are ready, bear down," the operator chimed in.

Bailey swept Eva's soaking wet hair out of her face as she prepared to once again push.

"EMS is five minutes away. Help is on its way, Eva."

Things moved pretty quickly after the baby's shoulders popped out, exactly the way the woman on the phone said it would.

"Holy shit," I repeated in awe of the life being born. "Push, Eva, keep pushing she's almost out," I guided, witnessing what I could only describe as a phenomenon.

"Grrrr…"

"That's it, you got this," Bailey soothed, rubbing her shoulder.

My thoughts ran rampant, thinking about the day I watched my mother die. Hating, resenting, blaming God. And there I was witnessing the miracle of birth, His creation come to life before my eyes. I was powerless to hold back the unexpected rush of emotions with seeing Eva's daughter being born into this world, playing a vital part in her birth. It was as though *he* was showing me his blessing in all forms.

Proving he didn't solely end lives, he started them too.

Just as the thought occurred, I grabbed onto the baby with the towel in my hands. Instantly hearing, "Wah! Wah! Wah!" loud and bold in the air. Immediately making her presence known.

I futilely tried listening to what the operator was saying, but I was held captive by the baby girl in my arms. Knowing I was the first person to ever hold her was an imprint I'd never forget. Almost like I was in God's plan all along, and he was making up for taking my mom all those years ago.

Everything that happened next was in slow motion. The paramedics rushed in, tending to Eva as I held the baby close to my heart. Locking eyes with Bailey who had tears streaming down her face. It was only then I noticed I had tears falling down mine as well.

That day changed my life in ways I never saw coming, making me a better man.

I wanted this with Bailey.

A baby girl.

A family.

A life of my own.

When she really started fussing, I brought her closer to my face, muttering in her ear, "It's alright, it's okay, I got you. I got you. You're safe."

One of the paramedics gently grabbed her from my arms and I immediately felt a huge sense of loss. Minutes later, I decided to ride with Eva in the ambulance to the hospital, not wanting to leave her alone, already having an attachment to that baby girl. While Bailey followed in my car.

Once everything was settled and we were in the hospital room, Mario declared, "You did great, Aiden. They told us they'd never heard anyone stay so calm before. I think you may have found your calling, son."

My eyes locked with Eva's who was beaming from ear to ear, holding baby girl in her arms. I would be lying if I said I wasn't shocked as shit when she added, "Mario and I would be honored if you would name her."

I jerked back, blown away by their request. "Are you sure?"

"Absolutely. You know we've been going back and forth for months on a name. I think it's because God had other plans," she vowed what I'd been thinking. "So would you do us the honor, Aiden?"

"I'd be honored," I simply stated, walking over to her. Baby girl opened her eyes as I rubbed her little hand, facing that strong connection to her once again.

I replied, "Faith. Her name is Faith."

Not only did she restore my faith in God, but she also gave me an immense sense of purpose. This was what I wanted to do with my life, I wanted to help people.

Deciding in that moment, Mario was right.

I wanted to be a doctor.

Nineteen

Camila

Now

"Two dirty martinis and three cider beers!" a customer called out from the end of the bar.

"Hey, can we get some service down here?" another hollered from the other end.

"Where are our drinks? Move your tits, sweetheart!"

"Come on sweet cheeks, been waiting fifteen minutes!"

"I ain't your sweet cheeks, cowboy. Just for that you'll be waiting ten more." I moved toward a different customer. "What can I get for you?"

Later that night after my run in with Dr. Pierce, I walked into Danté's club. Desperate for the distraction that bartending and dancing always provided. Needing to clear my head, focus on anything other than the Pierces.

Specifically, their father.

The man was never far from my thoughts for the rest of the day.

The look in his eyes, the sincerity in his words, the dominance and devastation he exuded, it all tore into me. Bit by bit.

How could I explain things I couldn't begin to understand?

I hated this. I hated this so much. The worst part was there was nothing I could do to fix it.

The way he looked, the way I felt, the instant connection that brought me to him. There was no denying it on my part, I wanted to know him.

Badly.

"Camila, Mamita!" Danté shouted, calling me over to his office.

I stood by the door with my arms crossed over my chest, leaning into the threshold.

"What's up with you tonight?"

"Nothing."

"It don't look like nothing."

"Why do you think something's up with me?"

"Cuz you ain't shakin' your ass. That ain't the Latina I know."

I scoffed out a chuckle.

"So spill, what's goin' on? What did Cheech do now?"

"It's not Jackson this time."

"Ohhhhh gurl, the tea just got *hot*," he exclaimed with a big smile across his face. "You are sizzlin', let me sip that tea."

I rolled my eyes.

"What did Doctor Daddy do? Put you over his knee and spank you?"

"Well that escalated quickly."

He smacked the air and grinded his hips into his leather chair, rocking back and forth to the beat of the music thumping through the walls. "Did he get all up in there, examinin' your booty?"

"Danté!" I scolded, standing upright.

"Gurl, don't pretend like you haven't thought 'bout it. Now that we know his wife is dea—"

"We don't know that."

He eyed me skeptically, pointing in between us. "Camila, who you playin'? You were in their master bedroom wit' me. You saw what I saw. That man's wife is long gone."

I sighed.

"What's up wit' you? Did you accidentally see his dick or somethin'? Ugh," he made a disgruntled face and noise from the back of his throat. "Is it small?"

"Oh. My. God." I shook my head. "Why do I even bother trying to talk to you?"

"Miss Thang, you haven't said shit."

"I saw him today." I simply replied.

"Oh…" he sympathized. "So it is small."

"Danté, be serious for one minute please."

"I am," he chided, weaving his head. "Havin' a small dick ain't a good look for a man that fine. Are his fingers at least long? How 'bout the tongue, how that look?"

"Oh. My. God!" I repeated, rubbing my forehead. "I didn't see his dick, okay?"

"Oh, so you're upset you didn't see it?"

"Danté, this has nothing to do with Dr. Pierce's dick."

"Damn, Mamita, that's a shame."

"Are you going to listen to me now?"

He beamed in that Danté sort of way, leaning back into his chair, he threw his bedazzled feet up on the desk. Nodding, "Proceed."

I took a deep breath, trying to gather my thoughts before sharing, "I think there's cameras in the house."

"Gurl..." He stuck his hand up in the air with nothing but attitude. "Don't tell me that, cuz I did not look my best that day. Had I known I would have—"

"Anyway, I lost my shit... I mean like legit lost my shit on a bunny."

"Come again?"

"I ended up leaving Journey with Jackson and drove their car to the hospital."

His eyes widened. "I think I need some popcorn." He pretended to throw one in his mouth. "Go on."

"When I got there, I met his RN Renee and she knew me. Like knew things that only cameras could see, so now I know there are cameras."

"Oh, gurl, have you been shakin' dat ass on camera with Paris these last few months?"

I shut my eyes, throwing my head back against the door frame. "Don't remind me."

"And the plot thickens. Doctor Daddy has probably been whackin' it off to ya, honey."

Ignoring him, I continued on with my story. "So, I stepped off the elevator on the floor where his office was located, and I swear to God, Danté, I felt him."

"Say what?"

"*I know*. It makes no sense, but I did. I felt him, I smelled him, I-I-I-I don't know … I just … I knew where he was before I even saw him. Like what the fuck is that?"

"Camila, that's some soul mate shit right there. Gurl, you gonna have his babies. What did he smell like? A man, right? A musky, sexy, doctor man."

Disregarding him again, I stated, "He's an asshole."

"Oh, baby, they all are. Especially dem doctors, thinkin' they God's gift wit' huge egos and cocks—"

"But then… I saw him in his office, and he was… he was breaking down…"

"Like breakin' it down?"

"No, like devastated. He was upset and then he threw his wedding photo."

"At you?"

"No, at the wall."

"Why?"

"I don't know."

"And then he slammed you up against that same wall and did you next?"

"Danté! We didn't do anything. He didn't even know I was there."

"So, he didn't feel you, but he probably saw you on the cameras?"

"Yeah."

"Then he's going to know you went to the hospital."

"I mean, I guess. I haven't thought that far ahead yet."

"Cuz you're thinkin' of his dic—"

"I have feelings for a man I've never met. My married employer. I'm not that woman, Danté. I will never be that woman."

"Honey, it don't matter. His wife is dead."

I wanted to argue with him, put up a fight for what he was saying, but I couldn't get my mouth to release the words. I knew deep down he was probably right, and that was the hardest pill to swallow.

"What kind of feelins'? Like I want you to be my baby daddy? Or like I'll let you stick it in my as—?"

"Intense feelings. Like I want to know everything about him."

"Includin' the size of his dick."

"No."

"No?" he sassed, calling me out on it.

"I don't know."

"Well, let me ask you dis. If you knew for a fact his wife was dead, would it be game on for you?"

"No. Yes... Ugh ...this is so confusing. At first it was just about the kids, and now it all shifted in a direction I wasn't prepared for."

"Camila, for you to even be interested in a man outside of Sean is surprisin'. He's the only guy you've ever been wit', and he did you dirty, honey. In and out of the bedroom."

I bit my lip.

"I guess that means Doctor Daddy has been the one leavin' your favorite things?"

I shrugged. "Or his nurse, Renee."

"If it was her, why wouldn't Skyler tell you? Why keep it a secret?"

He was right, and my heart skipped a beat at the thought of Dr. Pierce taking the time to do all that for me.

"Oh, Miss Thang, you like him," Danté hummed. "I can tell by the look on your face, he's makin' your heart flutter, honey. Baby, sit on Dr. Pierce's face and let that man make your puss—"

"The fuck," Sean seethed, making my entire body seize up. His tall, controlling demeanor standing behind me. His rage burning a hole in my back. "I know you ain't talkin' 'bout another man fuckin' what's *mine*."

I abruptly turned, locking eyes with him. "I. Am. Not. Yours."

"Says who?"

"Me."

"Like your opinion fuckin' matters to me."

"No shit, Sean. *Hence*, why we're not together."

"I'm the only dick that's ever been inside you. I claimed you a long time ago, and don't you ever forget that."

"See, this is why we always had problems. You treat me like I'm your possession. I'm nothing more than a trophy to you."

"Do you have any idea how many women would get on their knees for that title?"

"Yeah, too many to count, and that's only based off of the women who did while we were together."

"They meant shit to me."

"Well, they meant a lot to me. *Your queen,*" I mocked in a condescending tone. "What I do with my body is none of your business."

He stepped into my face, cocking his head to the side. "I'm makin' it my business."

Danté stood up fast, making his chair crash into the adjacent wall. Bringing our attention over to him, where his hand was firmly placed on top of the knife on his desk. Only glaring at the brick house next to me.

Sean eyed him up and down, scoffing out, "Bitch, please, sit your ass down." He slid open the front of his leather jacket, showing off the gun tucked in his jeans.

I didn't back down, this was Sean to a T. He had to solve everything with violence. I wasn't scared of him, I knew he wouldn't hurt me or Danté. Knowing how important he was to me.

"Sean, I'm warning you. Unless you want my heel up your ass, back the fuck up. Now."

He cunningly grinned down at me, grabbing ahold of my chin. "I love it when you're fuckin' feisty."

Yanking my face out of his grasp, I demanded, "Leave me alone. I don't belong to you, and I never will again."

"Try me, Camila. Just fuckin' try me and watch what happens to that fuckin' doctor. It'll be your fault he ends up in his own fuckin' hospital."

I stood taller, accentuating every word, "Are you threatening me?"

"No, baby." He snidely smiled, backing away slowly, never breaking his predatory stare from mine. He had the last word, spewing, "That's a fuckin' promise." Turned and left.

"I hate that motherfucker. Why did you date him again?"

"Because I didn't know any better."

It was the truth. I was so young when we first got together. I was blinded by my friendship with him, thinking it was love, when it was nothing more than lust.

"You alright?"

I spun, looking at him. "I don't know anymore."

"Camila, you gotta do what's right for you. Fuck Sean."

"And Bailey? What about her?"

"I think it's time you find out the truth, don't you?"

He was right.

The time had come.

There was no way around it anymore, not with the way I was reacting to him. If she was alive, there was only one thing left for me to do. It would be the right move, even if it killed me not to see those kids anymore.

I had to *quit*.

Camila

Now

I walked into the Pierces' home bright and early the next morning, a false sense of security following me. As soon as I stepped into their house, there was this eerie presence all around me.

I took a deep, sturdy breath, grounding myself. The sensation of being watched was very much alive and present, much more than it had been before.

For the life of me, I couldn't shake it.

Maybe because I was now convinced there were cameras, or maybe I just had a sixth sense for these sorts of things. Or it could have been as simple as I was starting to lose my goddamn mind. I hadn't slept all night, thinking solely about the Pierces. The image of their father breaking down in front of my eyes was a vision I couldn't forget.

The more I looked around his house, the more I saw her, the more I felt her, the more she presented herself to me.

His wife.

Bailey. Beauty. Mrs. Pierce.

I didn't know a damn thing about her, but she was everywhere. From the floor to the ceilings, in every crevice of every room, in every inch of the open space, in every way, shape, or form. This was her home.

Her sanctuary.

Her place of peace.

Her safe haven.

Where I suddenly felt unwelcomed. An intruder, a woman who wasn't supposed to be raising her kids. The more I looked around her home, the worse I felt. It was a continuous, unforgiving impression in the pit of my stomach, as if I had done something wrong and it was about to catch up with me. The confusion and unanswered questions pegged me as I moved through the house, picking up after the boys like I did every morning.

Except, this time…

When I walked into Journey's room to make sure she was still sleeping, Jackson was holding her in his arms in the rocking chair. This was the first time I'd ever seen him hold her, let alone look down at her with so much love and adoration.

I smiled. "You're a natural, Jackson. You're going to make a great daddy one day."

His eyes flew to mine, declaring, "I don't want kids."

"You say that now but you're so young. You have a full life ahead of you."

"I wouldn't talk about things you don't know, Camila," he snapped in a harsh tone.

My hands surrendered in the air. I learned early on I needed to pick and choose my battles with Jackson, and this was one I'd let slide for another time. I didn't want to ruin this moment between us. Journey looked so happy in his arms, pulling at her brother's shirt, holding onto him tight. She didn't want to let go.

It was a beautiful sight, one that had momentarily replaced the uncertainty in my mind.

Now that I had his attention, I addressed the elephant in the room, "Thank you for covering for me yesterday. I really appreciate it. You didn't have to do that for me."

"I didn't do it for you, Mary Poppins, I did it for Journey."

I nodded. "Well, maybe you also did it because you're starting to accept me?" Rocking on my heels, I added, "You know, maybe even like me?" I waited on pins and needles for his response. "A little, not a lot. Definitely more than you like Harley," I teased, hoping it would tear down some of his walls. Even if it was only for a second.

"You're right, I hate Harley."

I arched an eyebrow. "Do you, though?" I was treading on thin ice, at this point I didn't have anything to lose but everything to gain when it came to him and our dynamic.

"What are you trying to say, Camila?"

"Nothing, just an observation."

"Ah, so the same girly bs she tells me all the time."

"Which is?"

"I'm mean to her because I like her."

I shrugged, smirking. "Do you?"

"Fuc—"

I glared at him.

"F-u-c-k no."

I laughed, I couldn't help it. This little shit was such a smartass.

"You girls watch way too many Disney movies."

"Says the guy who has a few in his room."

It was his turn to glare at me.

I once again put my hands up in the air in a surrendering gesture. "What? I didn't put them there."

"Neither did I."

I didn't have to ask to know what he was implying. "I can move them if you want."

He narrowed his eyes at me, searching for something in my gaze before snipping, "Yeah, whatever. Did you find my dad?" he questioned, changing the subject to another discussion I didn't want to have.

"Kind of."

"Was he working?"

"You could say that."

"His precious hospital is all that matters to him anymore."

"I don't think that's true at all."

"How do you know? Did you talk to him?" There was no denying the hopefulness in his voice, breaking my heart a little more.

"I could just tell."

"How?"

"I could see it in his eyes. He misses you as much as you miss him."

"I don't miss him."

"Jackson…"

"I don't. I don't need him. To hell with him." There was so much pain in his words, making my heart bleed for him.

"You don't mean that. You're just angry. Trust me, I know what that feels like."

"You think you know everything, don't you, Mary Poppins?"

"I know I've become your punching bag, and I don't care what you tell yourself, I know you don't hate me. But if it makes you feel better to take stabs at me, then so be it. Hit me again, Jackson, because maybe there'll come a day when you can see me as your friend and not your enemy. I'm actually a pretty cool person. If you gave me half a chance, you'd see I'm not a threat to you. To anyone for that matter. I'm not here to replace anybody, I just want to help you."

"And then what? When you're done helping, you what? Just leave us behind?"

"Is that what you want?"

"No."

I smiled, thinking I got through to him. He abruptly stood, quickly handing his baby sister over to me.

"Journey wouldn't like that. Because let's face it, Camila, we both know she's the only one who wants you here."

I grimaced, and for the first time I saw regret pull at his eyes.

"Did that make you feel better? Because the expression on your face says otherwise."

With a spiteful tone, he bit, "Everyone leaves, that's just life."

My eyes watered, knowing in the core of my stomach he was referring to his mother.

"I'm sorry, Jackson, I hate that you feel that way. I wish there was something I could—"

"What did he say? I want to know what my father said to you."

Before I knew what I was responding, I blurted, "That he loves you very much," I unintentionally lied through my teeth, peering down at Journey, who was staring at me as intently as her brother, listening to every word I spoke like she needed to hear it too.

I couldn't look at either of them, my eyes shifted every which way and all across the room until they finally landed on Journey's favorite book *On the Night You Were Born*. Giving me the courage to speak up for him, "Your dad is hurting, and he just doesn't want you to see how bad."

"He is?" He genuinely sounded shocked.

"Yes. He broke down."

"In front of you?"

"Mmm hmm."

"After he said he was hurting?"

"Sort of."

"So, my father who'd just met you for the first time, willingly told you all this?"

"Mmm hmm."

"Why do I feel like you're lying?"

Our eyes connected.

"Why would I lie?"

"You tell me."

"I am telling you. Why is it so hard for you to believe your father loves you?"

"I don't know, Mary Poppins, maybe because I haven't seen him since my mom—"

"There you are," Skyler interrupted. "Jackson, you're going to be late for school. You gotta go."

I was going to scream.

Why was it every time someone was going to say something about their mother, they were interrupted? What. The. Hell?

Jackson grabbed his backpack off Journey's floor and walked out of the room, taking the truth of their mother's whereabouts with him. I shook off the thought, leaving it in the back of my mind for later.

"Camila, do you mind staying over tonight? I know it's Friday, but Jackson and Jagger are both staying with friends, so it will only be Journey and you."

"Bah!" Little Miss enthusiastically exclaimed, leaning her head on my shoulder.

"Girls night, huh?"

She kicked her legs in excitement.

"Sure, I don't mind."

"Great. Noah wanted to take me out, it's our anniversary."

"Awe, happy anniversary. How many years?"

"I don't know, forever."

I chuckled. I never did Google Skyler's name, it was her story to tell me. It didn't seem right reading it on online and not hearing her experience from her own mouth. I knew one day she'd tell me.

"He claims I've been his since we were almost twelve."

"And you haven't?"

"No, I have. I just like to mess with him. My husband needs to be kept on his toes, it's the Jameson in him."

"Is he anything like Harley?"

"Harley is her father, who is ten times worse than my husband, even though they're brothers. She's also a lot like her mom, Mia, too. I swear, Camila, the day Harley starts dating, oh man… I'm already sorry for that boy because Creed and Noah are going to kill him. I'm not joking, they're going to put him to ground."

I instantly saw Jackson's face, something was going to happen between them. It was only a matter of time, I was certain.

"They can't be that bad," I expressed, not feeling sorry for him. The little shit deserved it. Karma. He shouldn't be so mean to her in the first place.

Skyler gave me a stern expression as if she was thinking the same thing I was. "You have no idea. Harley may not be Noah's kid, but she was the first baby girl in the Jameson family, and for that fact alone, she has two fathers. And don't get me started on her grandfather Lucas and Uncle Mason, on top of the good ol' boys who are all assholes with hearts of gold. You'll meet everyone eventually."

"I can't wait."

"You know what? You should come to one of our MC barbeques."

"MC?"

"Yeah, motorcycle club. My husband is VP and his brother Creed is the Prez. Everyone would love to meet you, they've already heard so much about you from me. The whole family is as grateful for you coming into the Pierces' lives as I am. You'll fit right in like Aiden. He may own a Harley, but he refuses to join the MC, much to Noah's complaints, but it doesn't take away how much we all love him."

Aiden has a Harley?

"My husband never had a good example of a father, and Aiden stepped in when he was fifteen and took on that role. For that alone the family is thankful. They owe a lot to Aiden for saving Noah in a sense."

Hearing her speak his name, had my already overly active mind spinning out of control. Leading me back to wanting to know every last detail about him.

I casually probed, "Is Dr. Pierce grateful I'm here too?"

"Of course. I'm sure wherever Bailey is, she is as well. You've been a godsend, Camila."

"Skyler, where is Mrs. Pier—"

Her cellphone rang, cutting me off.

"It's Noah, I have to run. We'll catch up tomorrow." She kissed Journey on the forehead. "Have fun with your favorite person."

"Bah!" she replied, agreeing with her.

Skyler left, leaving me disappointed.

"Journey, do you know where your momma is?"

"Bah, gah, bah, bah, bah, dah."

"Is that right?"

"Fah, gab, bah."

"Does that mean you want a cookie?"

Her head bobbled.

"You're so smart. You know what, Little Miss, I think your brother wants me here too, but he's just too stubborn to admit it. What do you think?"

She bobbled again, more adamantly this time. She didn't have a clue what I was saying, however it still helped me.

It was funny how a baby could do that.

How holding her in my arms just made everything right in my world. The attachment I had to Journey grew with each passing moment.

We spent the rest of the day playing, dancing, and singing while music played through the speakers. I ignored the sensation of being watched and just enjoyed my time with her. She was standing by the edge of the coffee table holding on, bouncing to the beat.

"Go, Journey, shake your booty! Go, Journey, shake your booty," I cheered, and she did just that. Sticking her diapered butt out into the air, she wiggled it back and forth, a proud look on her face. My girl wasn't just copying me, she had rhythm. Music was part of her soul like it was in mine. "That's it, Little Miss, now shimmy like this." I showed her, moving my shoulders.

She giggled, trying to move hers without falling. I giggled right along with her.

"Now make your booty bounce, now make your booty bounce!"

"Boo! Boo! Boo!" she twerked it, vibrating her entire body, making both of us fall into a fit of giggles until she fell over from laughing so hard. I fell with her.

"I love you, baby girl."

Her eyes lit bright and wide, and I knew she understood what I said. She opened mouth kissed my cheek, grabbing onto my face hard. Displaying just how much she loved me too.

It was a little past nine o'clock at night when I got her to fall asleep for me, laying her down in her crib.

I whispered, "I'll see you in the morning. Sweet dreams, my angel," kissing her goodnight. Turning on the white noise, I grabbed the monitor and shut the door behind me.

For the next hour, I cleaned up our mess from the day, deciding at the last minute to pick up Jackson's room before I relaxed on the couch for the rest of the night. It didn't take me long to tidy up his things. For once his room didn't look like a bomb went off in it. And for some reason, part of me knew he did that for me.

The entire time I cleaned, the Disney movies on his shelf were calling my name, especially the one titled, *Beauty and the Beast*. Unable to remember the last time I watched it.

"Why not?" I asked myself, grabbing the video cassette.

I walked into the kitchen, tossed a bag of popcorn in the microwave, overlooking the fact it was my favorite.

Beep. Beep. Beep.

Pulling my favorite water from the fridge, I threw the caramel popcorn into a bowl and made my way into the living room. Laughing at the thought they were the last family on earth to still own a VCR.

After popping in the movie, I grabbed the remote off the coffee table and plopped my ass on the couch. Tugging the throw blanket on top of me, I settled in. Getting nice and cozy, excited to watch one of my favorite childhood movies. But the excitement quickly came to a halt.

My heart dropped.

I stopped breathing.

My eyes zeroed in on the screen in front of me.

There they were.

A young Bailey with Aiden down on one knee, stating,

"I'm just keeping another promise to you, Beauty."

AIDEN

Then: Eighteen-years-old

Bailey glanced up from her book when she heard the loud exhaust from my finished muscle car pull into the driveaway. I revved the engine just to get her going, she loved when it vibrated against her body in the seats.

With a huge smile on her beautiful face, she set her novel aside on the porch swing she was sitting on. Appreciating the powerful sound the pipes made.

Only staring at me, she remarked, "Well shit, happy birthday to me, handsome." Wiggling her eyebrows, she gazed at my elegant suit, similar to what Beast wore in the Disney movie.

I grinned, walking up the rickety steps slow and steady so she could get a good look at me. Nothing was better than turning Bailey on.

"What's with the getup?"

Placing her gift beside the swing, I sat down next to her, and pulled her into my lap.

"I'm going to get you all wrinkly."

"Like I give a fuck," I rasped, needing the warmth of my girl in my arms.

She straddled my waist, not leaving any room between us. Grabbing her chin, I brought her pouty lips over to meet mine, kissing her like she was the only thing that ever mattered.

She was.

A soft moan escaped her lips into my mouth, making my dick twitch in my tight slacks.

"What's gotten into you?" she breathed out against my lips. "You're never one for PDA."

"It's my girl's birthday."

"That's a mighty big package you have … does that mean I get everything I've ever wanted?"

I grinned, side-nodding to the present next to us. Knowing that wasn't what she was referring to. "Go put it on for me, and you'll find out for yourself."

She smirked, puckering her lips. "Is it lingerie?"

"Fuck that. Like I would ever make you mine in this fucking shithole."

"You're the only guy I've ever met that can say something so romantic with the words fucking shithole in the sentence."

"I live to please you."

"That you do, Aiden Pierce."

"Now go get dressed for me, Bailey Button. Not to be confused with belly button," I teased.

"Ugh … how many times are you going to say that lame joke?"

"After today, who knows."

Her eyes dilated and she bit her bottom lip. "Aiden, what are yo—"

"You're wasting time."

She grumbled, "Can I just have a hint?" Her hips rocked into my cock.

"Beauty, you're dry fuckin' the shit out of your hint right now."

"Oh, I see." She peered down at my tan vest, straightening up my gold tie. "We're playing dress up I take it? Does that mean I'm Beauty?"

"You already are."

She giggled, immediately reaching for the bag next to me. "I'll be right back."

"I'll be waiting."

Little did she know, this would be the last time she ever stepped foot into this sorry excuse for a house.

I sat there alone on the swing, swaying back and forth. Closing my eyes, letting my mind wander. Reflecting on how we got this far with all the obstacles we faced together and apart.

Every tear.

Every heartache.

Every disappointment and accomplishment.

That brought us together in the end.

Bailey was the best thing that ever happened to me. All that mattered was to make her happy, she was my sole purpose in this world. My gift sent down from my mother.

"You'll find someone who will always be there for you."

"I will?"

"Yes, I swear it."

"How do you know?"

"Because, Aiden. I'll personally send her your way. I promise."

The sound of the door hinge tore me back to the present. I wasn't nervous, hadn't been up until this point. The second I saw Bailey emerge from the entryway moments later, wearing Belle's gold princess gown, I nearly lost my shit.

She was stunning.

A goddess.

A vision that took my goddamn breath away.

Her long silky gloves went up past her elbows. Her brown hair was pinned up in curls on top of her head with the rest cascading down her back. The costume jewelry that hung from her neck and wrists reflected off the sun setting over the trees. Rendering me fucking speechless.

She was the spitting image of a Disney Princess. No longer the spunky little girl with pigtails, offering me the only food she had left all those years ago.

"This is too much, Aiden. Even for you."

I twirled my finger, silently ordering her to parade around for me.

She blushed, hiding back a huge smile as she picked up the sides of her dress to sway her thin waist right to left. Spinning in a circle, letting the gown follow her every move effortlessly.

"Goddamn, Bailey … the things you do to me."

She bit her bottom lip, "Ditto. So where are we going, Beast?"

I stood up, adjusting my cock in my slacks.

"Aiden!"

I was over to her in three strides, whispering in her ear, "I will never be able to watch *Beauty and The Beast* again without getting fuckin' hard for you."

She took my arm, trying to hide her bright red face in the crevice of my shoulder.

I laughed and kissed the top of her head, leading her down the stairs to my car. After helping her get in, I took one last look at her before shutting the door. Rounding the front of the car, never taking my eyes off her. I jumped into the driver's seat, grabbed ahold of her hand, and slowly removed her left silk glove to place small kisses up her arm. Ending my wake right below her ear where I sucked her lobe between my teeth.

Groaning, "You ready, Belle?"

She looked at me with nothing but lust and love in her eyes, simply nodding her response.

When I turned the key in the ignition and the engine roared to life, I baited, "Feeling wet, baby?"

Swiftly, she turned her shy expression toward the window, triggering me to scoff out a chuckle.

Shaking my head, I drove away from our past, cruising toward our future. This surprise took months of planning to pull off the perfect eighteenth birthday. I held her hand the entire drive, anticipating her reaction like a kid on Christmas. Wanting to make this a day she'd never forget.

Once we arrived at our first destination, I helped her out of the car, interlocking our arms once again. It didn't take her long to realize where we were, the woods we shared our first kiss in.

"I can't believe you brought me back here. How am I going to walk through the fallen trees and bushes, wearing this dress?"

"Easy"—I leaned forward and threw her over my shoulder—"I'm carrying you."

Huffing and wheezing, she looked over her shoulder. "This is not how princesses get swept off their feet, Aiden."

I smacked her ass. "No shit, this is how men do it."

"You're such a guy!"

She had no idea what I had planned. This wasn't the end, this was only the beginning of our day ahead.

As soon as we reached the same spot we shared our first kiss, I softly set her down. Grabbing onto her arms until she found her footing in the heels she was wearing.

"Oh, Aiden..." she muttered in pure amazement, looking at all the white string lights I hung in preparation for the day.

Twinkling.

Shining.

Sparkling.

There wasn't a tree or branch in sight that wasn't layered in white lights. Making it look like our very own little fairytale at dusk. They were everywhere and all around. It was quite a spectacle now that it was almost dark out.

I had more money than I did over four years ago, the first time I did this for her. I spent a small fortune on these costumes alone from a locally owned costume shop, not to mention what I still had in store for her.

She slowly took a look around in awe of her surprise.

In amazement of me.

In wonder of us.

The second she turned back to face me, her eyes hit the ground where I was already down on one knee.

"Aiden..."

"I'm just keeping another promise to you, Beauty."

She instantly broke into tears, remembering the first time we met.

"I like the way Bailey Pierce sounds. What do you think?"

"I like the way Bailey Pierce sounds too, but aren't we too young to get married?"

"No silly! I meant when we're older."

"Oh." I thought about it for a second. "Like how much older?"

Now it was her turn to think about it for a second. "Like when we're eighteen. That's old enough."

"Okay."

"Aiden..." She giggled, twirling her hair in a big knot around her finger. "You have to ask me first."

"Oh, I do?" I scratched my head. "When?"

"When we're eighteen."

"Okay." I nodded, meaning it. "I'll ask you when we're eighteen."

"Okay." She nodded back. "I'll try to act surprised too. Ask me in a good way, alright? So I cry."

She was confusing, but in the best way possible. I'd say anything she wanted just to keep her by my side, so I'd always feel this way.

Safe.

I knew right then and there my momma had something to do with this. I didn't know how, but she kept her promise to me. This had to be the girl, I felt it in my bones.

"Why would I want to make you cry?"

"Because they're happy tears and crying with happy tears is like super romantic."

"Oh... Okay then. I'll ask you in a way that will make you cry happy tears."

"Okay good, but don't make me cry in any other way than happy tears. Ever. You promise?"

"I promise."

"Those are happy tears, right?"

She fervently nodded and even with makeup running down the sides of her face, she was still the most beautiful woman I ever laid eyes on.

"They say everything is about timing, Bay, and I've waited years for this day."

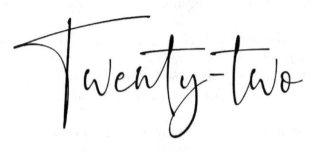

AIDEN
Then: Eighteen-years-old

Her mouth trembled as she licked her lips, captivated with every word I was expressing. Pouring my heart out to her.

"I can't tell you how many times just thinking about this moment got me through my darkest hours, Bailey. Seeing your face, your smile, your goddamn beauty. You're the light in my life. The love in it as well. You're the reason I'm still breathing, I'm hopeless for you now."

She smiled through her tears, flowing freely down to the ground in between us.

"Wherever you are is home to me. Do you understand me?"

"Yes," she sniffled, blinking away another tear.

"I can't live without you. You're my heart, Bay. You'll always be my heart," I stated, clearing my throat, getting caught up in this moment.

"I know. You're mine too, Aiden. Life has been hard for us, but I wouldn't change it for anything because it's what led me to you."

Her words couldn't have been closer to the truth.

"I just want to give you everything you ever wanted, including my last name."

She laughed, wiping away more tears.

"You're the beat in my heart, the blood running through my veins… I can't promise you that tomorrow will be easy, or that there aren't rough roads ahead, but I can promise you that I will forever be there with you, standing beside you, holding your hand, loving you with everything that I am. I thank God every day for the gift that is you."

I grabbed her left hand with one hand and with the other I pulled out the ring box in my suit jacket.

"I want to wake up next to you for the rest of my life. I want to fall asleep with you in my arms every night. I want to start the life we've been dreaming of since we first laid eyes on each other. I want you, Bailey, that's all I want, you're all I ever wanted… Will you do me the honor of being mine forever? Will you marry me, Beauty?"

She nodded, sucking in air. "Of course, yes, yes, yes a million times over!"

Her eyes never wavered from mine as I slipped the ring on her finger.

"I know it's not the biggest diamond, Bay, but I promise I'll get you—"

She threw her arms around my neck. "It's perfect."

I didn't hesitate to hold her against me, claiming her lips. We stayed just like that for I don't know how long. Lost in one another's embrace. Thinking about the once in a lifetime love we shared.

"This is the best birthday ever."

"It's not over yet."

"What do you me—"

I nodded to the orchestra who were walking up, softly playing *Canon de Pachelbel*, and she burst into tears again.

The ordained minister and the videographer I hired, who'd been recording all this time quickly appeared behind them. There was no way I wasn't recording this moment in time for us to look back on, and our children to watch some day.

"Lovely to finally meet you, Bailey," the minister greeted, taking ahold of her hand. "Are you ready to get married, birthday girl?"

She nodded, unable to form the words to say exactly what we both were experiencing.

"Alright, then let's get started."

She was hyperventilating at this point, and it was the most adorable thing I'd ever seen. I grabbed her hands, bringing them up to my heart.

"Dearly beloved," he declared. "We are here to join this man and this woman into holy matrimony. Do you, Aiden, take Bailey to be your wife, to have and to hold, for better or for worse, for richer, for poorer, in sickness and in health, to love and to cherish, from this day forward until death do you part?"

Looking deep into her eyes, I stated, "I do."

"Now you, Bailey... do you take Aiden to be your husband, to have and to hold, for better or for worse, for richer, for poorer, in sickness and in health, to love and to cherish, from this day forward until death do you part?"

"I do," she murmured with fresh tears falling from her eyes.

"Then with the power vested in me by the State of North Carolina, I now pronounce you husband and wife."

Before he could say *you may kiss the bride*, I couldn't restrain myself any longer. I gripped onto the sides of her face and tugged her over to me, kissing her as my wife for the very first time in the eleven years we'd known each other.

Growling, I kissed her more aggressively than before. Our lips crashed together in a rhythmic movement as she returned the push and pull of my mouth. Needing me just as badly as I needed her. She melted in my arms, surrendering to me. Knowing how much I loved it.

"You're mine now."

"I've always been yours," she replied, kissing me one last time. Blushing when she realized we still had company watching us, but I didn't give a fuck.

They were lucky I didn't take her right then and there on the forest ground with the way I wanted her, now that she was officially my wife.

I was going to claim every last inch of her, from her heart to her pussy, it was game on now. But for *her*, I tried to play nice with them, though, there was only so much I could take.

I shook the minister's hand and tipped the orchestra, excusing us pretty quickly after their congratulations. Rushing out of there by throwing Bailey over my shoulder again to carry her back out to my car.

She laughed uncontrollably, waving goodbye and saying thank you for the beautiful ceremony. Apologizing for our quick departure after we exchanged our "I do's". I tried not to speed the entire drive to my last surprise, however that was easier said than done.

The little minx taunted, "Why are you in such a hurry, Mr. Pierce?" in my ear.

"I've waited what has felt like a lifetime to live out my fantasy. What brought on my wet dreams almost every goddamn night since I laid eyes on you. To spread you wide open and slowly fuck that sweet pussy that's been dry humping the shit out of me all these years."

"I really need to stop blushing when you say dirty things like this."

"No." I kissed her, keeping my eyes on the road. "Please, don't."

She smiled against my lips. "Where are we going, Mr. Pierce?"

"Home, Mrs. Pierce."

"What do you—"

Cutting off her question, I pulled into a private driveway just off the main road. At first glance she saw the white picket fence, red door, and sunflowers growing all along the property immediately aware of what I was up to.

"No..." She shook her head, shifting her eyes to me. "You couldn't have."

"Oh, but I did."

We were in an older neighborhood, but it was safe, and we were together which was all that mattered. The one-story ranch was simple, modest, and all I could afford at eighteen years old. With the help of Eva and Mario, we renovated a few things on the inside.

"What? How? Oh my God!" She beamed, flinging the car door open. Running up the gravel walkway. I followed, catching her by the waist as she slipped on her heels, scooping her up in my arms before she fell.

This time, I carried her over the threshold of our new home the way a husband was supposed to. Stepping foot into the house I bought solely for her.

For us.

"As much as I would love to see your face while you look around our new place, I'd rather watch you come from my cock inside your sweet fuckin' pussy way more. The tour will have to wait till after, and by that, I mean sometime next week, baby. Cuz I'm not leaving your body till I am damn ready to."

She smirked, batting her lashes.

Once we reached the master bedroom, I set her down. Not paying any mind to our surroundings like she was.

There was a queen-size mattress in the middle of the floor with clean sheets and pillows on it. A small side table with a single lamp, and Eva's mother's old wooden rocking chair that had intricate designs carved into the back was placed in the corner. She insisted I take it, saying it would bring us luck for when we had children of our own. She even draped my old worn out Ninja Turtle blanket across it.

Our small Key Lime pie wedding cake was placed on a tray in the center of the bed. Bailey's favorite flavor besides me of course.

While she was lost in our future, I was focusing on the present. I walked over to the small radio on the floor and pressed play, and the soft tune of "Tale As Old As Time" strummed off the speakers in the room.

Bailey's eyes lit up like Christmas, turning to face me. "Aiden... Oh my God..." was all she could manage to say.

I placed one hand on the small of her back, pulling her petite frame in closer. Her hand found mine, intertwining and I rested them on my chest near my calm heartbeat.

Our feet started moving to the music, swaying us both along the old wood floor. We danced around our bedroom for our first dance as husband and wife, slowly gravitating all around the space.

"I love you, Aiden. I couldn't have asked for a better birthday, proposal, wedding, *home*... Oh my, how do you do it? How do you always outdo yourself?"

I twirled her around, drawing her back to me. "You make it easy, Bailey."

"I'm not going to lie, I'm a little nervous about what happens next."

"You mean about me making love to you?"

"Yeah ... I mean, what if I'm awful? What if I'm not what you expected, what if—"

I kissed her, soft and gentle, seeking out her tongue before backing away to spin her again. I spun her a few more times, engraining the memory of her in that gown in my mind.

Wearing it for only me.

On the last twirl, I stopped when her back was to my front, and slowly slipped the zipper down on her dress. Admiring her beauty, her silky skin, the way my lips glided along the side of her neck. She leaned into my chest, beckoning me to keep going.

"Bailey Pierce," I rasped into her ear, causing shivers to stir on her flesh. "You were made for me, and don't you ever forget that."

Her gown pooled at our feet in a heap of gold silk fabric, as I continued stripping her bare. In one swift movement, I was down on my knees, kissing along her thighs, up to her sweet spot. Getting her nice and ready for what would be our first encounter of love making. By the time I was done devouring her heat, she was soaking wet.

A moan escaped her pouty lips when I abruptly stood, removing all my clothes. Laying her down on the mattress to kiss my way up her body. Looking profoundly at her until we were face to face. Our connection searing its way into our souls.

"I love you."

She panted, "I love you too."

I would forever remember this moment as the first time everything was right in our world, because we finally became one…

As husband and wife.

Twenty-three

Camila

Now

My heart was in my throat, proceeding to watch such a private moment between two people, who were obviously madly in love with each other. Simultaneously, an uncontrollable surge of emotions rushed over me with a sudden queasiness settling in the pit of my stomach.

I found it hard to take a breath, let alone inhale multiple breaths trying to maintain my afflicted composure.

What was this reaction for a man I barely knew and hadn't met?

My mind began churning with uncertainty, mimicking the contents of my stomach as it rose to the back of my throat.

My core sped up with each word that fell from his lips, from his heart, from the place inside of him that only belonged to her.

"I can't live without you. You're my heart, Bay. You'll always be my heart."

And from every word that fell from hers in the same place she resided.

"I know. You're mine too, Aiden. Life has been hard for us, but I wouldn't change it for anything because it's what led me to you."

Tears started pooling in my eyes, clouding my vision, my judgement, my goddamn mind.

My heart sped faster…

My thoughts even faster.

A whirlwind of sentiments ran over me, leaving a trail of urgency behind.

I felt the happy tears running down her face as if they were my own.

Was I crying?

Why was I crying?

He wasn't mine to cry over.

It was like I was her and she was me. An eerie shiver hit my body hard. I could physically feel her happiness, her joy, her love...

Their love.

Their pain.

The need to be wanted, needed, adored just the same.

It was right there in front of me, unfolding in the depths of my soul. This picture-perfect couple, their fairytale and happy ending I'd imagined in my mind so many times, I lost count.

What they looked like together.

How they spoke to one another.

The sounds of their voices and the way they were with each other.

It was as beautiful as it was devastating to endure. The way he worshiped her, the way she returned the devotion. What I thought didn't even compare to what I was seeing before me.

What I was experiencing on their journey of becoming husband and wife.

I stayed there like that, frozen in time. Sitting at a standstill with them. Lost in a world where true love prevailed. The laughing, the smiling, the unity of what they were. Living, breathing, it was all real around me.

I needed to move, I needed to get up and turn it off, I needed to do a lot of things, but I couldn't get my body to move. Not an inch or for a second. I had to experience it with them whether I wanted to or not.

It wasn't right. It was wrong. What I was doing was so very wrong.

I sat there battling an internal struggle, my heart was going to explode. It was beating uncontrollably. I was there but I wasn't.

And *then*...

Everything went cold.

I felt *him* before I even turned around to face the consequences of my actions. For watching his proposal, his wedding to a woman who wasn't here.

Where was she?

Where was Bailey?

It was the never-ending question the man behind me could only answer.

I felt his misery.

His agony.

His isolation and despair.

I felt it all, stabbing a knife into my back. Over and over and over again.

My hand immediately went to my chest, my heart breaking, shattering to the ground. Only emphasizing where fragments of his laid next to mine.

Nothing could have prepared me for the sequence of events that happened next. The unbearable weight of his demons were beyond my control. I surrendered to them.

I surrendered to *him*.

Longing for the resolutions in a situation I still had no idea about. He wanted to brand me with his devastation, and there I sat willingly taking every marking. It gave me comfort in a place I knew was about to turn ugly.

"You're the beat in my heart, the blood running through my veins... I can't promise you that tomorrow will be easy, or that there aren't rough roads ahead, but I can promise you that I will forever be there with you, standing beside you, holding your hand, loving you with everything that I am. I thank God every day for the gift that is you."

More tears slid down my cheeks, adding to my frazzled state. The desire to fall apart was there. I was on the cusp of losing a battle I wasn't equipped for.

No weapons.

No armor.

No protection against the deafening silence standing guard at the far side of the living room behind me.

"Will you do me the honor of being mine forever? Will you marry me, Beauty?"

"Of course, yes, yes, yes a million times over!"

I shut my eyes like a child watching a scary movie. Terrified of what surprise was going to jump out, of what would happen next.

I wanted to scream…

To run…

To hide…

But that wouldn't change anything.

I was there … he was there … and for the first time we were finally going to meet.

I dug my nails into my skin, trying to take away the pain he was suffering. Anything to take away the hurt I felt, having to endure his worst nightmare.

My mind shouted, "Turn around, Camila. Just turn around and face him … ask him everything you want to know … ask him what you deserve to know! Call him out for being a shitty father. For not being there for his kids that still needed him. For the responsibility he shoved onto me…"

Abruptly finding the courage, I turned and opened my mouth at the same time the minister on the video declared, *"Dearly beloved."*

I couldn't form words.

I couldn't think.

Not when he was watching the video in front of us as if he was there with her and not here with me.

Even with the dim lighting of the room, I could still see his glossy eyes, his trembling lips, the entranced expression on his handsome face. I was spellbound by him while he was enraptured in her.

"We are here to join this man and this woman into holy matrimony. Do you, Aiden, take Bailey to be your wife, to have and to hold, for better or for worse, for richer, for poorer, in sickness and in health, to love and to cherish, from this day forward until death do you part?"

He looked so stunning and tortured all at once. Not blinking, not breathing, not moving an inch to the point his heart may have stopped beating.

"I do."

It wasn't until the minister repeated, *"Now you, Bailey…"* Did his eyes lock with mine.

I gasped ever so slightly, this over-whelming, powerful, all-consuming connection to this man was staring intently into my eyes. He felt it too, I could see it hidden beneath his torn walls. They were splitting down the tight seam, exposing a side of him that had my heart breaking all over again.

There was something familiar about him trying to break through, but I couldn't pinpoint what it was. His eyes burned with a ferocity that had me in a trancelike state.

I couldn't breathe.

He was confining the air right out of me, as I watched snap shots of his life like a movie reel playing within his eyes.

Every question I had, every uncertainty, all the anger, the resentment, the downright determination was gone in a flash.

I wanted to give him everything I had. Everything inside of me. I would have given him every last part of me to change the look in his stare.

It was killing me.

Fresh tears slid down the sides of my face, and I sucked in a breath, holding on for dear life. Without words, he was showing me the deepest part of him.

His oldest wounds.

His jagged scars.

His regrets.

His life...

And the damage it all left behind.

"For better or for worse, for richer, for poorer, in sickness and in health, to love and to cherish, from this day forward until death do you part?"

"I do."

Her response echoed in the room, vibrating off the walls. Although the spell between us didn't break until we heard, *"Then with the power vested in me in the State of North Carolina, I now pronounce you husband and wife."*

His gazed faltered first. The fire that once burned in his eyes seconds ago, singed to ash and was replaced by an icy glare. The man transformed, and the beast came to life. He scowled coldly and crudely at me, like I was the witch who put the curse on him.

Seething...

"How fucking dare you?!"

Camila

Now

His fists white-knuckled at his sides.

Slowly and cautiously, I stood from the couch, surrendering my hands out in front of me like that would somehow make things better.

"I-I-I-I-I…"

He was in my face in one second flat, towering over my petite frame like a hungry wolf, biting, "You what?"

I instantly stepped back in panic, a natural reaction when a threat was looming near. My heel connected with the coffee table behind me, losing my footing. My arms flew up in the air to steady my balance, but it was useless. I was going down fast and hard until his warm hands caught my arms in an overly tight grasp. Holding me upright, inches away from his vicious stare.

Through a clenched jaw, he gritted, "Do you not know your place in this house?"

"I'm-I'm-I'm—"

"You are *nothing* but a glorified babysitter who does a shitty fuckin' job cooking and cleaning my home."

My breath hitched from his accusations. His menacing eyes narrowed at me as he worked his jaw in anger.

Cocking his head to the side, he crept closer to my face. "If it weren't for Skyler, I would have never hired someone like you. You don't know how to respect people's privacy. Parading around with your fuckin' friend when you were supposed to be tending to my kids!" he roared, making me jump out of my skin.

I went to move, but his grip tightened on my arms. Holding me defenseless while his heated anger rolled off his shoulders.

"Do you make a habit out of breaking into people's personal property? I should really have you arrested for this."

I jerked back. *What the hell was he talking about?*

"You had no right going into my safe and getting that video out! Let alone sit here with fuckin' popcorn like you're at a goddamn movie."

"Wha—"

He growled, silencing me. "How the fuck did you even know the code?"

"I-I-I-I—"

"For fucks sake just answer the question!" His eyes read of irritation. "I don't have time to listen to your stuttering mouth."

Oh hell no.

"That's right … you don't have time for anything right? Not even your own children."

He didn't even flinch. I thought he'd let go, but he didn't. If anything, he held on firmer, wanting to prove to me or maybe himself he was still the one in control. My eyes gravitated to the flickering light coming from the TV still playing his wedding video. Casting a dark shadow on the adjacent wall that kept growing taller and taller over mine.

"What I do with my kids is none of your goddamn business! Do you understand me? Or am I not making myself crystal fuckin' clear?"

"Excuse me?"

"You heard me."

"You have it all wrong, Aid … Dr. Pierce. I didn't go into your safe. I didn't even know you had a safe… I found the video in your son's bedroom, while I was doing a *shitty job* picking up after him. It was in *The Beauty and Beast* case. I had no idea. Watch the surveillance videos you obviously have *hidden* all over the house, if you don't believe me."

"That didn't stop you from watching what wasn't yours to—"

"What do you expect from me? I have been here for over three months, taking care of *your* responsibilities and I've yet to meet my employer, but you know what? Now that I have, I can see why your kids can't stand you."

He let me go, backing away. I didn't know if it was for my protection or his.

"I'm not going to fight with you." I turned to leave but he grabbed my arm again, pulling me back toward him.

"Then I suggest you don't walk away from me!"

I snapped, "Then stop screaming at me," trying to stay calm in a situation where I wanted to lose my shit on him. "How dare you speak to me like that?"

"Listen, Cami, I can speak to you how I damn well please. Last time I checked, *you* work for *me*."

"My name is *Camila*," I stated, emphasizing each syllable in my Spanish accent.

"I don't even know how to fuckin' pronounce that."

"Here, *repeat after me* … Ca-mi-la."

"Now who's been watching who?" he countered, referring to his argument with his staff at the hospital.

"At least I can admit it."

"Oh, I can admit it, *Cami*. I've been wondering how long you've been off the pole."

"Sabes que…" My eyes widened, taken back. "Eres un puto cabrón!"

"The fuck does that mean?"

"It means you're a fucking asshole!"

"I've been called way worse, sweetheart, but maybe it's time I wash your mouth out with soap?"

"Wow. How much have you been watching me?"

"Whenever Doctor Daddy needed to fuck his fist, yeah? Isn't that what your friend said?"

"His name is Dan—"

"I know what his name is."

"Then learn how to use it."

"How cute, you actually think I give a damn about what you want. I think you're forgetting who works for who. Do I need to remind you, *Cami*?" He stepped toward me and I instinctively took a step back, missing the coffee table this time, but that didn't stop him.

"All you've done is disrespect this house, my home, the one my wife and I..." He paused, halting his steps. Just as quickly as the thought came on, he shook it off. His broody demeanor coming toward me again.

Step.

Step.

Step.

Until my back hit the door.

He swiftly caged me in with his arms, eyeing me up and down with an expression of authority. Hovering over me, making me feel so small.

"Hiding things about our kids, coming to my hospital, prying in our bedroom, fighting with our son, and let's not forget you shaking your ass like you're a goddamn whore in front of our daughter."

"That's not—"

"I don't want to hear your pitiful excuses. My kids deserve better."

"You're right. They deserve their parents. Where is their mother, huh?"

For a second his eyes glazed over, but he simply blinked it away.

"Answer me! Where is the woman who should be taking care of her baby? The mother who is missing all Journey's milestones? Do you both even know what she looks like anymore?" The palms of my hands connected with his chest, giving him a shove.

He didn't falter.

"Did you know she can pull herself up on furniture and has taken a few steps along it? Do you know how many teeth she has now? Or here's a good one... What's her favorite song to be sang to her?"

His chest heaved the further I pushed every button of the truth I've been dying to say to him for so long.

"That's what I thought! You have no idea! You call yourselves parents? Watching from afar on a nanny cam isn't parenting, it's neglect. Maybe YOU should be arrested!"

Without missing a beat, he got right up in my face again, snarling in a menacing tone, "You're fired! Now get the fuck out!"

"What? No!" I shuddered, fervently shaking my head. "You can't do that! You can't fire me!"

"I. Just. Did."

"No! You can't do this! Journey needs me! And Jackson and I were just turning a corner—"

"Well then, turn your ass around and get the fuck out of my house!"

Before I knew what was happening, he yanked me away from the door, manhandling me. He grabbed my purse off the entry table, opened the door, and tossed it out on the lawn. The contents went everywhere, including my cash and phone.

The tears pooled in my eyes. Threatening to surface when he shoved me out the door next.

My voice.

My heart.

My very being was falling apart.

But I still managed to say, "Please don't do this … at least … let me say goodbye to them," I expressed with a shaking breath. "I love them like they were my own."

He took one last look at me with callous, beady eyes, scoffing, "Well they're not. You don't belong in their lives or this house."

The door slammed in my face with no compassion or regard for how I felt. Leaving me with nothing.

No answers.

Especially, about his wife.

AIDEN
Now

I stood there.

My chest heaving.

My heart hammering.

Losing my fucking mind.

I was the beast.

She didn't deserve any of the bullshit I just spewed or how I treated her. She was the only reason our home was becoming united again after so long.

"Goddamn, it, Bailey," I whispered to myself, battling like hell not to open the door and allow Camila everything she craved.

Including *me*.

I felt it.

Our intense connection.

From the second she stepped foot into this house for her interview with Skyler, I was drawn to her...

A woman who wasn't my wife.

I couldn't do that to Bailey, to our marriage, to the love we shared.

I wouldn't.

It was one of the reasons I hadn't met Camila. On top of the several other circumstances I existed outside of this house. The walls were closing in on me, and I found it hard to catch my breath. Feeling her everywhere...

And I wasn't just talking about the woman who would forever own my soul. The love of my life.

Beauty.

It didn't stop me from watching Camila on video every chance I got. Seeing her bond with Journey, her struggle with Jackson, her attention to Jagger, all of it since day one. Her devotion to my kids, to this house, to their lives held me captive every day. The least I could do to show my appreciation was to buy her favorite things she casually mentioned to Journey.

I may not have physically been here for my children, but I made sure they were safe, fed, and had a roof over their heads. It was all I could manage to do. I was stuck in the past, unable to move forward or think about the future. My life had been ripped away, but my kids were always on my mind.

No matter what, they were there.

I had become a shitty fucking father, I knew this. I let down my family in unforgiveable ways for circumstances beyond my control. Abandoning my kids and home to pour everything that was left of my existence into the hospital. The one place I didn't feel her or see her. I became the man I always promised myself I'd never be. I couldn't even look at myself in the mirror without seeing all the shitty foster dads staring back at me.

I was one of them.

Once I heard Camila start walking down the steps and away from our home, my chest tightened to the point of pain.

Squeezing…

Choking…

Suffocating what was left of me.

I took a step, about to open the door and allow life to run the course it was set to follow. Damning me to Hell for disrespecting my wife but giving my children what they absolutely needed.

Her.

I turned the knob just as Journey's loud wails began resonating down the hall. Another problem I wasn't ready to face quite yet. My feet still moved on their own one right after the other, pushing my body toward her nursery.

Skyler and Journey were the only ones who knew I came back every night after twelve-hour shifts. Checking on the kids while they were sleeping. I felt like a piece of shit every time I saw Camila sleeping in the guest bedroom with my baby girl in her arms.

Jackson was so mad at me. *His father*, the same one who'd always been his hero turned into one of the biggest disappointments in his life. He was acting out in ways I should have expected, though. Camila was handling it like a fucking champ. He was putting her through the ringer, and she took each and every blow. Giving it right back at him. My son needed a role model, and she was proving to be exactly that.

Jagger was withdrawing more and more into himself. My second born had always been quiet, reserved, thought shit out before he spoke. Wiser than his years. Bailey used to joke he was born an old soul, taking after me...

His father.

I couldn't stay away from my children. I was there the only way I knew how, by watching from afar. Although neither of us deserved it, I lost count of how many times I saw Camila show Journey pictures of Bailey and myself, emphasizing we were her parents.

Journey knew me, she knew I was her daddy. I'd sit in the rocking chair that was supposed to bring us luck and watch her every night.

Anytime she was sleeping, she'd always wake up, even if it was only for a few seconds, she'd make eye contact with me and smile in her sleep haze.

There were several times she was already awake, waiting for her old man to show up.

Other than her, my sons hadn't seen me since the day Bailey left me over eight months ago...

I stopped living.

Breathing.

Surviving without her.

Not seeing her but feeling her was worse than fucking death. Every breath I took felt as if it were my last.

How do you mend a broken heart?

How do you go on with life without your person walking next to you?

I missed her so damn much. I wish she'd come back to me, to us.

As soon as I walked into Journey's room, she reached for me like she did most nights when she was awake. Standing against the bars of her crib.

Except I couldn't hold her.

I couldn't comfort her.

Our daughter.

Our baby girl.

The one we always dreamt of and prayed for.

I couldn't be the father she needed. The one they all needed. I didn't know who I was without my wife. Without her love, her reassurance, her smile.

I was lost in plain sight.

Journey wasn't having it tonight, though, like she knew I'd just fired and threw out her favorite person. She was throwing a fit similar to the ones she used to have before Camila held her in her arms and made her know she was wanted.

Loved.

Adored.

Her wails got louder, blocking out all my other senses. Her cries turned into ear-piercing screams, and still I couldn't reach for her, hold her, feel her against me.

"Baby, I'm sorry... Daddy is so sorry." I broke down, falling to my knees. Pleading for mercy, for forgiveness, for another life where Bailey was still by my side.

With me.

Beside me.

Holding my hand.

"I never wanted this life for you, Journey. It was never supposed to be like this. Please forgive me, I need you to forgive me."

More wails.

More screams.

More, more, more.

"God, is this what you wanted for me all along? I get it, okay? I hear you! Please I am begging you to make her stop. Please help me move on ... I can't live like this anymore. I can't go on."

I couldn't take it anymore. My resolve broke, loud and fucking clear.

Sobbing.

Aching.

Fucking dying inside.

Tears ran rapidly down the sides of my face as did Journey's. There was no end in sight.

"Please, God, just send me a sign ... please, I need something to hold onto..."

And just as I wanted to give up, surrender my goddamn flag, I heard Journey cry out, "Ma! Ma! Ma!"

My heart stopped.

My stomach dropped.

The room started spinning.

I felt her. She was there with me. With us.

The woman I couldn't for the life of me forget...

Vowing, "I'm here, Aiden, I'm here."

to be
Continued

The continuation of the Pierced Hearts Duet
Choosing You: May 14th

PREORDER HERE:

AMAZON
ITUNES
KOBO
NOOK

CPSIA information can be obtained
at www.ICGtesting.com
Printed in the USA
LVHW051454290419
615959LV00015B/1238